Rotten to the Core 3

Lock Down Publications and Ca$h
Presents
Rotten to the Core 3
A Novel by *Ghost*

Lock Down Publications
P.O. Box 870494
Mesquite, Tx 75187

Lock Down Publications
Like our page on Facebook: Lock Down Publications @
www.facebook.com/lockdownpublications.ldp
Cover design and layout by: **Dynasty Cover Me**
Book interior design by: **Shawn Walker**
Editor: **Sunny Giovanni**

Stay Connected with Us!

Text **LOCKDOWN** to 22828 to stay up-to-date with new releases, sneak peaks, contests and more…

Thank you!

Submission Guideline.

Submit the first three chapters of your completed manuscript to ldpsubmissions@gmail.com, subject line: Your book's title. The manuscript must be in a .doc file and sent as an attachment. Document should be in Times New Roman, double spaced and in size 12 font. Also, provide your synopsis and full contact information. If sending multiple submissions, they must each be in a separate email.

Have a story but no way to send it electronically? You can still submit to LDP/Ca$h Presents. Send in the first three chapters, written or typed, of your completed manuscript to:

LDP: Submissions Dept
Po Box 870494
Mesquite, Tx 75187

DO NOT send original manuscript. Must be a duplicate.

Provide your synopsis and a cover letter containing your full contact information.

Thanks for considering LDP and Ca$h Presents.

Ghost

Chapter 1
Jayden

My heart pounded in my chest like that of an African drum. Sweat poured down the side of my face, causing my shirt to stick to me. It felt as if the air was getting thicker, the closer I got to Janet's bedroom door. I looked over my shoulder again to make sure that no one was following me as Mary J. Blige continued to serenade the house with her rendition of "Sweet Thang". I wiped the sweat from my brow with the same hand that I was holding my .45 as I crept closer and closer to her bedroom door, already noting the fact that it was opened just a crack; enough for me to hear the loud moans, heavy breathing, and the constant squeaking of the springs from her bed.

I swallowed my spit as I felt another drip of perspiration slide down my spine, ending at my lower back. It felt like something was crawling on me, but I didn't have any time to focus on that. I had to keep a clear head. *Move forward with the task at hand*, I said to myself as I crept all the way to the side of the opened door and placed my back against the wall.

I took another deep breath, leaned forward and opened the door with my pistol just enough for me to see inside of Janet's room. What I saw nearly left me speechless. I bugged my eyes out of my head as my jaw dropped.

There was Nico— my former right hand man, my enemy, my target— lying on his back, while Janet held the top of the headboard, popping her back like a wild Bronco, riding him for all that he was worth.

Her supple breasts wobbled on her chest. Her thick ass cheeks jiggled, opened then closed, as she rode him faster and faster, causing the headboard to slam into the wall again and again, while he held her cheeks in his hands with his eyes closed tightly.

"Un, un, yes, fuck mama, Nico! Fuck me, baby! Fuck me! Ooo-a, ooo-a, un, un, unh, yes, aw shit, yes, baby!" She hollered, speeding up the pace.

I watched her pussy swallow his pipe repeatedly, from my vantage point. He grabbed a hold of her swinging titties, pulling on the nipples, causing her to tilt her head backwards with her mouth wide open, moaning at the top of her lungs. The scent of their romp was heavy in the air. It smelled like they had been fucking for at least an hour straight. Beads of sweat trickled down Janet's back, and Nico's forehead was as wet as mine.

I watched Janet lean all the way over, sticking her tongue into his mouth, while he rubbed all over her ass. She twisted her hip before slamming it forward, taking as much of his dick as she could. She moaned into his mouth before licking all over his lips as he spread her ass cheeks wide enough for me to see the crinkle of her little hole back there.

I was so transfixed by what was going on before me that I'd almost lost sight of the reason I'd come to Janet's house in the first place. I felt my pipe throbbing from the show they'd put on. It left me excited until I snapped out of it and curled my upper lip.

I trudged into the room after taking my .9-millimeter off my waist, aiming it and my .45 at the bed. "Well, well, well, look at what the fuck we have here," I said loud enough for them to hear me over the Mary J. Blige record. I cocked the hammer on both guns as I mugged them with internal hatred.

Janet fell off of Nico, leaving him lying on his back with his dick stuck straight up in the air. It was glistened in the dimly lit room, coated with Janet's forbidden juices.

Nico scrambled to get up, wiping sweat from his face, looking up at me with a mug and furrowed brows. "Bitch nigga, this how you getting down? I thought you wanted to fight it out to the death. I should've known you wasn't 'bout that life. Snake ass nigga!" He growled.

Janet fell to the floor and pulled the cover over her body with tears running down her face already. She bit on her fingernail, and I could see how badly she was shaking.

Kilroy ran into the room with both of his guns aimed at Nico. "Yo, you was right, kid. This fuck nigga is here. Hell yeah, you finna pay, son. Word to my mother." He cocked the hammers on his gun and looked from Janet over to Nico again.

I stepped forward and lowered my gun, angling it so that the bullet would slam into his shoulder first. I had visions of wanting to torture him first. Make him cry like a bitch for the way he'd murdered my mother in cold blood. I couldn't believe that we'd grown up together and had been nearly inseparable from the age of six on up to twenty-one. I'd never loved any nigga like I did Nico. He'd always been more than a brother to me, even though we weren't related by blood.

His mother, Janet, the same broad that was on the floor right now, was probably wondering if me and Kilroy were going to body her along with her son. She had always been like a mother to me, even though we'd gotten down in that bedroom on more than a few occasions. Shorty was a beast and had my lil' ass stretched out while she put that vet pussy on me time and time again.

We were all something like one big weird ass family, until me and Nico wound up robbing and knocking off his sister's boyfriend and father. That night we went on a high speed chase with the police, and only one of us was able to get away, so Nico insisted that it be him, and I didn't argue. I didn't wanna be locked in no box no way. That shit wasn't for me. But in exchange for him taking the rap for everything, he told me to promise that I would come up with his bail money, a good lawyer, and most importantly that I help his mother out with her bills, and never cross the line with his little sister, Whitney. I mean, I tried as hard as I could to stand on those promises for him. I got him a good lawyer that cost me fifty bands. I was ready to put up the cake for his bail, but then his probation officer went ahead and revocated him and stopped that from happening. I made sure that I paid up all his mother's bills for the entire year and kept her with at least a gee of pocket change at a time. But the one thing I could not do, as much as I wanted to, was stay away from his bad ass sister. Shorty was way too cole and had a body to die for, just like her mother.

As soon as Nico was behind them bars and out of the picture temporarily, my man's down low began to call out for Whitney, and unfortunately, she heard everything he was hollering loud and clear and responded in kind. It wasn't long before we were fucking all day and all night. We couldn't get enough of each other. That was until my cousin Myeesha came up from Atlanta on some jealous shit and broke all that up. But by that time, Whitney was already pregnant with my lil' one.

Kilroy ran over and grabbed a pillow from the bed, placing the barrel of his gun up against it before aiming the concoction down at Janet with his eyes lowered. "Yo, let me body this nigga, mama, like he did your Jayden. An eye for an eye, nah'mean?"

Janet crawled backward until her back was against the dresser with her knees to her chest, shaking her head. "Please, don't let him kill me, Jayden. Please, I've never done anything wrong to you. You're my son too." She whimpered with snot running out of her nose.

Nico slid his hand under the pillow to the right of him.

Boom! The .45 jumped in my hand when the bullet flew out of it and slammed into Nico's forearm, punching a big hole in it.

"Ahhhh! He grabbed his arm and fell off of the bed, holding it while blood gushed out, and oozed through his fingers. "You bitch ass nigga! Aww!" He hollered through clenched teeth. He took his discarded shirt from the floor and wrapped it around the gunshot wound.

Kilroy ran over and grabbed the .44 Desert Eagle from under the pillow that Nico was going for. He put it on to the small of his back and grabbed a handful of Janet's hair, wrapping it into his fist, then pressing the barrel of his gun into her temple. "Bitch nigga, you was gon' blindside me, huh? Well two can play that game." He looked down at Janet as she cried and whimpered.

"Please, don't do this, baby. Please. I'm not responsible for what my son did."

"Give me the word, Jayden. Let me waste this bitch, bruh!" He hollered as Mary J. Blige got to singing about a real love in the background.

I knew that she was Janet's favorite artist. There had been multiple times while I was hitting that cat that she'd have her crooning out of the speakers.

I held up my hand. "Not yet, bruh. Let me fuck this nigga over first, then we'll decide what we gon' do with her." I said still trying to get the nerve up to give the order for Janet to be put down.

I didn't know if I wanted her to die. Even though Nico had killed my mother, I still didn't have it in me to feel so cruel toward his. Especially since for as long as I had known her she'd been nothing but good to me. I honestly felt like she was the only mother that I had left, and Nico didn't deserve her. I know that might have sounded crazy, but it was my thinking at the time.

Nico slowly struggled to get to one knee, then started to stand up, wincing in pain. "Kill me, Jayden. Kill me and let my mother go. She ain't have nothing to do with this. This shit between you and me. We can handle this shit like—"

Boom! My bullet slammed into shoulder, knocking a huge chunk of meat out of it. He twisted around as the next two bullets plowed into his back, knocking him forward into the nightstand where he knocked the lamp to the floor, right beside his head.

I kneeled, turning my gun around and grabbing him by the throat. "Fuck I look like having mercy on yo' people when you murdered my mother, nigga?" *Bam!* The handle of the .45 slammed into his forehead, opening it so wide that I could see his meat on the inside. "Snitch ass nigga! You a disgrace to the slums of Philly." *Bam! Bam!* I slammed the handle into the same spot again, opening his gash wider.

Janet whimpered behind me while Kilroy kept her hair twisted into a ball inside his fist. "Please, don't kill him, Jayden. Please. I already lost Whitney. I won't have no babies." She cried. "Ahh!" She screamed.

Kilroy had picked her up and slammed her onto her back, before putting his gun into her mouth. "Bruh, we been in here too long. et's body they ass and get the fuck up out of here. Fuck this soft shit!" He hollered and I could tell that he was getting irritated and I couldn't blame him because usually when we went out to handle business we were in and out with no remorse.

I slammed the handle of my .45 into Nico's sunken face for the fiftieth time, then stood up, watching him slowly try to open his eyes that were already swollen and bloodied. "I used to love you, nigga. You was my dawg. But all things must come to an end." I curled my upper lip and pulled the trigger three times. *Boom! Boom! Boom!*

His body leaped into the air again and again, until finally he lay still with his eyes wide open and unseeing. I took a step back as our memories from our childhood began to play over and over in my mind. Sweat poured down my back and my heart felt like it kept on skipping a beat. "Let's get the fuck out of here, bruh." I said, shaking my head to snap out of the remorseful zone that I was falling into. I found it ironic that I hadn't felt any better after killing Nico. In fact, I felt worst because I knew that Janet would have to come next. There was no way around it.

"Yo, so I'm bodying this bitch then?" Kilroy asked looking up to me, and kneeling so that his knee was over her throat. Her legs kicked wildly up under him.

I rushed over to their side, kneeled, and kissed her on the cheek. "I'm sorry, mama. I swear to God I love you." I looked up at Kilroy and nodded, then jumped to my feet and hustled toward the bedroom door.

Boom! The bedroom lit up for the last time, and then me and Kilroy were running out of it, down the hallway, and then the stairs. I couldn't understand why my heart was so heavy as we ran down the alley at full speed toward our stolen getaway car, before heading back to DC. The whole way, I was too sick to utter a word.

Chapter 2

It was three days later and I was set to get the fuck up out of Philly. I had plans of moving down to Atlanta with my cousin Myeesha. I wasn't supposed to be there for more than a week before I would be put on to a lick that would gross me more than $2-million, and I couldn't wait. I'd heard some good things about Atlanta. That the women were strapped, fine as hell, all about their paper, and also that the niggas were grimy.

I got down for the cause and didn't like outsiders, but they were slower than us back in Philly, and I had plans on using that to my advantage. I was leaving the city with $750,000 of my own money, so I was good to go. I had my mind set on clocking as much paper as possible, and putting them niggas from the A on their heels.

Kilroy shook his head placing a kilo of heroin on to the table, and pushed it in front of me. "Here, nigga. This a parting gift from me. I would've had a few bands, but you already know I gotta rebuild the army. Now that you and Poppa gone, them Blood niggas trying to get the Shooters to plug in under their mob, but I ain't going. We gon' hit a few licks and be back up and running, nah'mean?" He said, sitting on the couch across from me, placing a .45 on the table in front of him.

I shook my head. "Nah, don't fuck with 'em like that. I already told you that I'ma send for you and the Shooters as soon as I get established. After I bust this first move, I'll have enough bread to get us a chapter down in the A. I just gotta make sure it's good, then

I'ma need my niggas down there fucking with me the long way. I'm trying to take over some shit. That's why I'm going down ahead of y'all. So this ain't me parting, it's me going to get us set up. Word is bond."

Kilroy shook his head. "You know the Feds snatched Naz's ass up straight out of the hospital bed. I hollered at son yesterday and he sick as fuck. He said to tell you to be easy, and to get the fuck outta dodge because yo' name ringing more than a trap phone. I don't know what Shawn gon' do now that he gone. I mean, I'ma look out for her as best I can, but I got a whole family to worry about on my own, nah'mean?" He reached onto the side of the couch and grabbed a bottle of Hennessy, twisted the cap off of it, and took long swallows from it.

I watched his Adam's apple move up and down before he put the cap back on to it, and burped all rude and shit.

Shawn was my cousin Naz's baby's mother. She and I at one point in time had been an item back in high school, but we wound up falling off over one summer. When my cousin Naz came over from New York, I hooked the two of them up, and shortly thereafter she'd gotten pregnant. It was then that I discovered that my cousin was a straight dead beat. That nigga didn't take care of her or their son, so I had to step in and up to the plate behind his back so I wouldn't bruise his ego. Well, after a while, Shawn and I began to get a little friendly, until I was waxing that ass. One day while we were doing our thing, Kilroy's right hand man, Poppa, caught us in the act, and said that we'd have to admit to my cousin Naz what Shawn and I had done.

I knew that wouldn't fair well. My cousin, Naz, was a complete cold-hearted animal with no remorse. Had he found out about me and his baby mother, he would have for sure killed his baby's mother, their kid, and probably tried me as well, though I was sure I would've knocked his head off because he was more impulsive than a thinker, and if any true goon was going to survive in the slums, you had to be a thinker over everything else. But instead of going through all that, or risk finding out what he would have done, I wound up bodying Poppa in the alley, while we were on a mission to handle some business with some niggas out of Virginia. After wasting him, I kept the $500,000 that he'd brought in order to fulfill his part of the drug transaction. Then I made it look like the niggas had set him up and took his paper. The slums were crazy.

"Yo, don't even worry about Shawn. Before I rollout I'll make sure she's good. Then, I'll hit her every month from down there. Make sure you let the homey know I got his family on my back. Word is bond. You just make sure you keep his books nice until I send for you kid, aiight?" I stood up and walked around the table, pulling Kilroy into my embrace and giving him a half of hug, patting him on the back. "I love you, son. Never forget that." I kissed him on the cheek and held him tighter, meaning every word that I said.

Ever since we've been in tune with each other, he and I had caused hell, side by side. Sometimes when I thought about the fact of me killing his right hand man, it made me feel some type of way, but I would then quickly shake that out of my mind because I had to do whatever I had to, to survive in the jungle amongst killas like myself. It was a crazy game, but it was what it was.

Kilroy nodded. "Son, I'm giving you a few months and then me and the Shooters will be down there, ready to get money. Until then, we gon' rock from DC and give Philly a breather so them Alphabet boys can focus on another mob. The kid ain't trying to be in the can for nobody. I'm holding court in the streets of the homeland. Word is bond. That's on my daughter." He said, hugging me again, and shaking his head.

"Yo, a few months is all I need. I'll be in touch. Hold ya' head, son. Love," were the last words I said to him before left, stuffing the kilo of heroin into my knap sack.

***

I knocked on the back door for the second time, then placed my ear to it after looking over my shoulders, praying that nobody was watching me. I frowned, took a step back and looked at the back of Shawn's crib, just as the curtain moved. "Man, Shawn, get yo' ass down here and open the fucking door!" I hollered, feeling my temper begin to rise because I didn't like being out there knowing that the Feds were probably scoping their house. All I wanted to do was to get inside so I could see what was good with her and my lil' cousin. I kept on looking over my shoulder, paranoid, thinking that at any moment the Feds were going to jump out at me.

Finally, I heard the lock coming off of the back door. Then, it opened slowly, and Shawn stuck her head out. "Come on in, Jayden. I'm sorry, I was inside taking a shower." She took a step back so I could get past her.

I tried my best to fix the mug that was on my face, but couldn't help how irritated I was. I could smell the scent of her body wash as I walked past her. It smelled like strawberries. "It's good, I just know them people lurking around somewhere, and I just wanted to come over so I could make sure you're straight before I leave Philly." I said, walking into the upstairs door, looking over my shoulder at her.

After she stepped into the house behind me, she locked the door and looked up at me with sad eyes. "I still can't believe you're leaving, Jayden. What the hell are we going to do without you? It's going to be so hard." She whimpered, lowered her head and walked up to me, wrapping her arms around my neck.

I placed my hands onto her hips and kept them there, even though the scent of her was doing something to me. She had on this real thin, silk night gown that was short enough for me to see her thick thighs. I already knew that she was strapped and had been ever since we were in high school. It was one of the reasons I had snatched her up to be my girl back then to begin with.

She looked up and into my eyes. "Can't you just take me and lil' Naz with you?" she asked softly. "I mean, you wouldn't even know that we're there. I'd do anything that I could to make and keep you happy. You have to know that." She said, stepping on her tippy toes and kissing my lips.

My hands trailed and cuffed that fat ass booty, rubbing all over it and pulling up the gown along the way until my hands were on hot flesh. I moved them lower, feeling into her hot crease, taking my finger and running it up and down her slit. Pressing and entering her hole, I felt it suck at me as if it were hungry.

"Unnn, I knew you had more than one reason for coming here, Jayden." She popped back on her legs and spread them, giving me all the access that I needed to do my thing. "Un, un, un, un, fuck Jayden, you so nasty." She moaned.

I fingered her with two digits, sliding them in and out of her at a rapid pace, feeling her get wetter and wetter while I sucked on her neck, tasting her skin. I'd always had a thing for Shawn, and just because she had a baby by my cousin, that didn't make it go away. Shorty was too bad. "Let me wax this shit, ma." I said, picking her up.

She wrapped her legs around me, and we crashed into the wall of her kitchen, right next to the stove. She sucked all over my neck, then licked it up and down, while her robe opened to reveal more of her naked breasts with the big brown nipples. "You know you can have this pussy, Jayden. You can have this pussy whenever you want it. Just take me with you. Please. Unn, shit, baby!" She hollered, throwing her head back.

I had my hand under her ass, playing all in that pussy, feeling her juices drip off of my right wrist.

"Fuck me now, Jayden. Stop playing and fuck me."

My pants fell down to my ankles as soon as I unbuckled my Gucci belt. My dick was already rock hard and sticking out of my boxer hole, throbbing in the air, ready to hit that pussy that was supposed to belong to my cousin. I couldn't wait to feel that heat. So as soon as I felt my head separating her sex lips, I clenched my teeth and lowered her on to me. Inch by inch, her pussy swallowed my pipe until she inhaled the whole thing. I bent my knees just a little bit and got to bouncing her, noting that her robe was completely around her waist now. Her titties bounced with milk leaking out of the nipples. Seeing that shit turned me all the way on. It was like it made it that much more forbidden to me.

I got to slamming her on my dick, harder. "Huh, huh, huh, huh, huh, huh, huh, uhhhh, hell yeah!"

Shawn's mouth was wide open with her eyes closed. She licked all over her lips, and in my opinion she had never more sexy than she had in that moment. "Umm, umm. Fuck me, Jayden! Yes, baby, un, un, un, ooo-a, shit!" She wrapped her legs around me tighter, threw her head forward and bit into my neck so hard that I couldn't hold back any more.

I got to bouncing her faster and faster as I felt my seed building deep within me. Her juices ran out of her hole and dripped off my balls. Her walls sucked at me and squeezed me as tight as a fist.

She dug her nails into my back and screamed loudly into my ear, "I'm cuming, Jayden! Awww-shhiittt!" She growled, throwing her head back again.

As soon as she started to cum, I smashed her into the wall, sucking the milk off of her nipples, popping my hips forward faster and faster, and then I was coming hard while my body jerked again and again. The whole time her walls pulled at my pipe, milking me, sending tingles through me.

I was getting ready to lay her on the kitchen floor so I could hit that pussy with her knees to her chest, when the house phone rang. I found that odd because I didn't know most people still had house phones and land lines and shit when they had access to better technology.

Shawn's eyes got bucked. "Oh my God, that's Naz. He said he was going to call me at three o'clock this afternoon." She unhooked our connection and got to her feet, running in the living room, grabbing a cordless phone and putting it to her ear after pressing a button on it. Then, she pressed another one, and another one a few seconds later. "Hey, daddy! How are you doing? I miss you so much." She cooed into the phone.

I pulled my pants up. My dick was still throbbing harder than before, and now I could smell the scent of her pussy on it. That made me feel some type of way. I walked into the living room, holding him in my hand. I stroked him while I looked over her pretty ass titties. Her nipples glistened from my saliva and the milk that leaked out of them.

"Yes, daddy, I'll make sure that I do exactly that." She lowered her head. "I haven't been doing anything. I've been in this house, missing you, and wishing that you were here with me and your son."

I walked up to her and grabbed a handful of her hair in one hand, and fed her my pipe. She sucked it into her mouth, bobbing her head while looking into my eyes, before popping him out.

"I love you too, Naz, you know that." She licked around my head, stroked my dick in her little fist, then sucked him into her mouth, and got to deep throating it like a pro while I felt all over her titties, humping into her mouth, looking down on her. I watched her jaws hollow in and then out again. The vein in her neck looked more prominent. She slid her hand into her lap and started to play with her pussy, sliding two fingers into herself and running them in and out. "Yes, daddy. I'll be there, don't you worry." She said into the phone, then sucked me back into her mouth.

My eyes rolled into the back of my head as I felt her nip long my penis head with her teeth, just enough to drive me insane. I pulled my dick out of her mouth, and it caused her to make a loud sucking sound. She swallowed her spit, just as I lifted her and slid under her to sit on the couch. Then, slowly, I guided her back and onto my pipe, watching her sex lips separate before swallowing me again.

"Yes, okay!" She squeezed her eyes together, bouncing in my lap, biting into her bottom lip while my hands smushed her titties together, and I humped upward into her womb again and again.

She dropped the phone and reached to pick it back up. Soon as she bent over, I really got to fucking her as hard as hard as I could while she whimpered and bit into her bottom lip. Her ass cheeks jiggled as they crashed back into me. I spread my feet and went as hard as I could until I felt my balls get tight, and hen my seed was spilling out of me and into her box.

* * *

After she got off of the phone, and we finished another round, I sat on the couch with her on my lap, kissing all over my neck. I had a few hours until I was thinking of rolling out of Philly, and I just wanted to spend them with her so I could clear my head. "So, anyway, that ten gees on the table is for you and Lil' Naz. I'll make sure I send you something every week, and if I forget, just hit me up and I'll make sure I get that right to you. I ain't gon' leave you alone out here, that's my word."

She kissed my cheek, then nuzzled her face into my neck. "It should've been us, Jayden. You and I. I would have been so happy with you. I know that for a fact." She took a deep breath and exhaled loudly. "I love you so much, and you better send for me. I'm not playing either."

I nodded. "Like I said, when I get situated, and find out what city I'm going to, I will, but not before that. Until then, you just let me know what you need, and I got you. I promise." I said that to her and I meant every word of it. I would not allow for her to struggle. I already knew it would be hard to raise a child on her own. Especially in Philly where as a single black female the odds were stacked heavily against her. The best I felt I could do was to be there for her financially. I owed her at least that.

Chapter 3

I arrived in Atlanta, Georgia at ten o'clock that night and met Myeesha at the Greyhound bus station on the east side of the A. She pulled alongside my whip in a drop top, pink Bentley, with all white leather interior, and pink stitching around the seats. There was a small television in her wheel that had to be illegal. She also had one in her dashboard, and in each of her headrests. She stepped out of the Bentley wearing a pink and black Michael Kors dress, with all red bottomed heels, and as I got out of the car, she kicked her heels off and ran around until she got to me and wrapped her arms around my neck. She smelled like Chanel Number 5.

"Jayden, oh my God! I can't believe that you actually came! Fuck, I done missed you so much." She said, holding me tight, before taking a step back and kissing my lips all hungry and shit. She was breathing heavily, and the longer the kiss lasted, the more she humped her body into mine, until my piece was rock hard and threatening to bust through my pants.

I rubbed all over that ass, massaging the cheeks while buses pulled into the depot, and people got off and onto them. The air was real humid, and bugs were flying all around us. I looked around the parking lot to make sure that we weren't being watched by none of the locals. I felt out of bounds and uncomfortable because it had been such a long time since I'd been out to the A. I knew niggas out there were real grimy, and stick up kids to the fullest.

Myeesha was rolling a Bentley, so I had to make sure that everything was good. I knew I couldn't confirm that just from looking around, but it eased my anxiety a little bit.

"I missed you, cuz, and I told you I was coming. We gotta get this bread. You know damn well I wasn't passing that up." I kissed her lips one last time, and brushed her long, curly hair out of her pretty face. "Why you wanted me to meet you at a bus station when I drove my own whip?" I asked, confused.

She took a step to the left and looked over my 1987 Chevy Caprice Classic, and raised her eyebrow. "You can't roll that no more." She scrunched her face and shook her head as if she were disgusted or something. She almost looked sick.

"And why is that?" I looked her up and down like she lost her mind. That whip had been with me ever since I first stepped off of the porch and started hustling. I had way too many good memories that were attached to that car. It was going to be hard for me to let it go.

"Because, nigga, you in the A now, and everybody down here rolling foreign, or nothing at all. I mean, you might get a way with a few old schools, but they gotta be decked out. That car right there is an embarrassment to you and me. You're in my world now, and I gotta get you up to par, lil' cuz. Let's roll." She waved for me to follow her. "Just leave that bitch running. Somebody will take it and do something with it." She rolled eyes and laughed.

I shook my head and ran to my whip to grab my two suitcases, and the duffle bag, before slamming the door back. I looked to my right and saw a heavy-seat, younger female loading her baby into a stroller after getting off of one of the buses.

I placed all of my things into the awaiting trunk of Myesha's Bentley, closed it, and jogged over to the young sista that I guessed was headed for a bus stop because she had one of the flyer schedules in her hand. "Excuse me, sista, are you about to get on the bus right now?" I asked, smiling down at her.

She started to fix her hair, taking a tuft of it and putting it behind her ear. "Yes, I am. Why? You got some bus tickets you trying to get rid of for the low?" She asked with optimal eyes.

I shook my head. "Nah, cutie. You see that black on black Caprice over there? That's mine, but I want you to have it so you ain't gotta be on the bus trying to get from point A to point B with your lil' one and all. Nah'mean?" I looked down at her baby girl and smiled.

She placed her hand on her hip and looked me up and down. "So, you just gon' give me a whip? Why is that?" She eye batted her lashes at me and licked her lips. I could tell she was choosing.

I laughed. "Yo, just felt it on my heart is all. Look, it's yours if you want it. It ain't stolen or nothing like that. All you gotta do is switch over the tags on your own time. The title is still blank. You take care of yourself, cutie, aiight?" I laughed again before jogging over to Myeesha's Bentley.

She was fucking with the radio until Cardi B's "Be Careful" started. She looked up at me with her MAC lip gloss freshly applied. "I know you wasn't over there trying pull ol' girl. What? You like chubby women now?" She laughed as I got into the car and close the door.

I shook my head. "I told her she could have my old whip. ain't want it to go to waste. I could tell that she could use it. Oh, and she was a cutie too." I adjusted the seat and nodded to the track bellowing out of the speakers. I glanced over at Myeesha's thick ass thighs that were exposed because of the short Michael Kors dress.

She grunted and nodded, before pulling out of the parking lot and stepping on the gas. Her long hair started to blow in the wind almost immediately. I still couldn't believe how bad she was. That often blew my mind. "I'm so glad you're here, and it's just in time too, because Percy doesn't get back into town for two days. By that time, you should have a complete understanding of what I'm trying to accomplish. It's a guaranteed two million in cash in it for you, and that's after what I'm going to be getting. I also wanna cash in on his heroin thing, and take command of the Queen of Spades club he just opened and gave me fifty percent ownership of. After we hit his stash, I think it would be smart if we venture out into some legit shit. You know, have that long-term paper that nobody can touch. We can't be in the streets forever. Sooner or later something is going to have to give." She turned on her left blinker and switched lanes.

I was fascinated by how smooth the Bentley cruised through the night. It didn't even feel like it was real, and that baffled me. I felt like we were on air, and the seats were super comfortable. I had to step my game all the way up. "Yo, if this nigga cutting you in on his dough already, giving you part ownership of his club, why the fuck are we layin' him down?" I asked, confused, because it seemed like she had it made. It didn't make sense to me for her to be greedy and hit a nigga for his shit, when it sounded like he'd hand it over long as she played her cards right.

She drove on to the highway and stepped on the gas, after putting the top of the Bentley up, and adjusting her seat so that it was back a little further. She turned down the Cardi B track, pulled a Dutch out of the ashtray, and handed it to me. "Here, light this."

I took a lighter out of my pocket, set fire to the Dutch, and took two deep pulls before handing it back to her. "Here. You tell me what's good." I wasn't about to let us lighting a Dutch distract me from what I wanted to know.

She pulled off of the cigar stuffed with Loud, inhaled and pulled off of it again before handing it back to me. "Aiight, peep. Percy is one of them nasty ass niggas who only cares about fucking as many bitches as he possibly can, while controlling them in every single way." She switched lanes in traffic, and turned the air conditioner up a little higher, adjusting the vent so that it blew directly on her. "I don't want you freaking out or nothing, or making a move too soon, but this nigga be beating my ass, Jayden, and I ain't talking no petty ass whoopins either. I'm talking, this nigga be fucking me up. Never in the face but everywhere else. It was also another one of the reasons I had to get out the A for a while." She took the Dutch from me and took four nice pulls before handing it back.

At hearing her tell me that a nigga had been putting his hands on her, my heart began to pound in my chest so bad that I could hear it in my ears. My vision grew hazy, and I couldn't stop from rolling my head around on my neck. I loved my cousin with all my heart, and I wasn't about to let no nigga put his hands on her in my presence. I didn't give a fuck how much money was at stake. It was my job to protect her over everything else. That nigga Percy was already on my shit list.

Myeesha shook her head. "Damn, I know I shouldn't have told you that. You over there steaming ain't you?" She blew air through her teeth and exhaled loudly. "Please just hear me out, Jayden, and we'll go from there, okay? I promise if you just keep a cool temper, we'll be rich." She looked over at me and attempted a weak smile.

"Yo, you already know you shouldn't have said shit, but you did, so let's keep it moving. Is that the only reason you wanna knock his ass off?" I asked, pulling off of the Dutch another four quick times with my jaws puffed. I inhaled, and closed my eyes, feeling the high take over me. I felt like I was in a movie or something. I felt good and mad at the same time.

"Well, when Percy come back, he and I are supposed to be getting married." She paused and looked over at me. "I guess I left that part out. I'm sorry, cuz."

I shrugged. "It's good. I mean, you ain't gon' be married to him for too long. Word is bond, son definitely gotta meet that reaper now." I tried to hand her back the Dutch but she waved me off, so I kept on smoking.

"If I can get this nigga to walk down the aisle with me, then whenever you do knock him off, I'll get everything, and you already know we gon' go hard. This fool got beef with all type of niggas in the A. Before his brother got indicted by the Feds, they had this crew that went around the A jacking niggas and putting them in trunks. It's how he acquired most of his money and businesses before he turned legit, but these killas out here ain't forgot about that. I feel like they're just waiting
on their moment. But before that moment comes, I need him to walk down this aisle with me. You feel me, lil' cuz?"

I nodded. "Most definitely. How long will it be until y'all get married?" I asked, dropping the Dutch roach out of the window and into the highway. I was high as a kite. I could barely keep my eyes open.

"Two months. Two months from tomorrow, on the fourth of July."

I licked my lips and nodded. "That sound like a long ass time from now. What am I supposed to do in the mean time?" I got a lil' irritated because I figured that we would be hitting his ass right away. I'd get them bands and send for Kilroy and my crew, then we'd take over some shit in the A. You know, make it the new Philly. I smiled at that thought.

Myeesha sucked on her bottom lip all sexy like, and looked into my eyes with her green ones, as usual leaving me kind of mesmerized. "Until then, I'm gon' need you to get under this nigga. Gain his trust and become his right hand because ain't nobody really fucking with him out here because of how his brother got down, so he looking for a killer that's a part of the family. And since he think I love him so much, I told him about you, and how you got down, and he was dying to meet you." She smiled and switched lanes until we were getting off and on to an exit ramp.

I shook my head. "You already know I don't like, nor fuck with most niggas. It's gon' be so hard for me to fake it with this chump. I'm gon' wanna body him every step of the way ahead of schedule, and you already know I ain't going if he try and put his hands on you in front of me. I love you too much for that shit. Word is bond, son's noodles will get punched out of his skull." I curled my upper lip at just imagining him touching my cousin. I swear I hated fuck niggas with a passion.

"Aww-uh, you so sweet and evil at the same damn time." She laughed. "But you ain't gotta worry about him crossing that line while you're in town. I gave that nigga your resume. He know what's good. Trust and believe me on that. Ever since I told him about you, he ain't laid a finger on me. I think he did his research and asked the streets of Philly what was good. He got a few connects out there that I'm sure put him up on who he was fucking with, so we should be good. However, if he slip up, then bust his brains, and we'll figure out another way." She looked over at me and smiled. "I love how crazy you are about me. That never ceases to amaze me, and it never gets old to see. I swear on everything that I love that I'm going to make sure that you're a boss as fast as I can. I know what you deserve, Jayden, and I'm gon' help you get it. I'm sorry about your mom, too. I hope you're getting better." She said, pulling along a winding path that led to some woods before it cleared, and we entered into Buck Head. She stopped at the lights, just as a police cruiser pulled alongside us and chirped his sirens.

I felt sick right away. I knew the car smelled like weed, and I had over $750,000 in the car, along with ten kilos of heroin and five of cocaine. Had it come down to it, I would have to burn the cop, but I hadn't brought any firearms with me, so I was stuck. "Yo, fuck this pig want, ma?" I asked, feeling my high leave me almost immediately. My throat got dry as well.

She smiled. "Chill, Jayden, it's good. It's just Felix. He patrols this area and probably wants to say what's up." She rolled down her window as the cop got out of the car and came around until he was looking down at her.

He pulled out a flashlight, and shined it in my face. "Myeesha, how are you doing today, little gorgeous one?" He asked, mugging me.

She smiled, reached out of the window and pushed his flashlight away. "I'm good, but can you not point that in his face like that?" She frowned.

He clicked it off and laughed. "Oh, that's my bad. But who is he?" He leaned on the windowsill and looked me over closely.

I could smell his Axe cologne and it made me sick to my stomach. I hated the smell of men.

She sucked her teeth. "He's my little cousin from LA. He'll be down here for a few weeks, then he's going to fly back west. His name is Mark, and he's studying to be a microbiologist."

Felix looked impress as he nodded. "Oh, wow, that's pretty cool. Well, Marcus, I hope everything works out for you. The world needs more Black scientists. That's inspiring to hear." He smiled then looked down at Myeesha. "Well, I guess I'll catch you at another time, gorgeous. Y'all be safe out here, ya' hear?" He touched the brim of his police cap, tilting his head just a bit, then turned and walked back to his cruiser, finally storming away. I ain't like his bitch ass already, and I didn't even know him.

Myeesha shook her head. "Don't trip off of him, Jayden. Right now I need to keep him close. He'll be an important tool that is used in all of this. Trust me." She pulled across the street and headed down a long road before it came to a big gate. She got out of the car and slid her card into a slot that was attached to a digital face, then she placed her finger against the screen, before the huge gate slid to the right, and opened. "Welcome to Sunnyvale's Gated Community." She laughed.

I was still heated at the fact that she'd told the cop my name was Mark, and his Uncle Tom ass had managed to turn that into Marcus as if that's what she really meant to begin with. I disliked Black people that were racist against their own. I hoped that I would get the opportunity to knock his head off somewhere down the line.

Chapter 4

I stepped out of the shower and closed the glass door behind me, stretching my arms over my head while my dick swung from right to left below my waist. Then I took a few steps forward until I was standing in front of a huge vanity that had six light bulbs along the top of it. It was so bright that I had to squint. Percy's mansion was laid out. The bathroom was so big that I was sure at least twenty people could've fit inside of it and get dressed at the same time. I looked over my naked body in the mirror, running hand over my abs, then flexing with my muscles popping out. I saw that I had to get my lining touched up, but my natural waves were popping.

I took the Burberry drying towel off of the vanity and wrapped it around my body, before leaving out of the bedroom and into the big bedroom. As soon as I got into it, Myeesha stepped into the bedroom wearing a small Victoria Secret nightgown that stopped just below her crotch. She softly closed the door behind her, smiling at me all seductive like. I couldn't help looking her up and down, stopping on her pretty toes that were painted pink and black to match her Bentley. She had so much swag that it was crazy to me.

"I see you couldn't wait to try that big shower out, huh?" she asked as she walked up to me, and rubbed all over my chest while she looked into my eyes.

I nodded. "I figured I had to get Philly off of me or I was gon' stay sick. I miss the homeland already. Word is bond."

She frowned. "Aww-uh. Well, at least you're here with me though. I mean, didn't you miss all this?" She took my hand, pulled up her short gown, and made me run my fingers through her fat, bald sex lips. She was already a little slippery, and that turned me on.

I rubbed up and down her box, looking into her green eyes that were lowered into slits. "Yeah, I missed this shit. So what you gon' do about that? You gon' introduce me to some southern hospitality or what?" I asked, slipping a finger deep into her body, pulling it out and sucking it into my mouth, tasting her salt, loving every bit of it.

She ran her tongue all over her lips, and then sucked on her bottom one. After pulling my towel away, she took a hold of my dick and stroked it. "Tell me what you want me to do, Jayden, and it's done. You wanna fuck me? You want me to suck this dick? Whatever you want, I'm down for it." She dropped to her knees, stroking my pipe, looking at it and making her mouth wet.

I placed my hand on her head and wrapped her curls into my fingers, just as she slid me into her mouth and started to suck me nice and slow, glaring her green eyes into mine. I humped into her mouth with my head tilted to the side. I had so many freaky things in my head that I wanted to do to her. So many that they were causing my brain to shut down. I had to snap out of it. "I want some of this pussy for sure, Myeesha. You already know what's good. You know you got that good-good." I said, pulling her up and laying her back on the big bed.

She placed both of her feet on the bed and pulled her gown back, exposing her naked, golden pussy lips. She took two fingers and separated her lips. I could see her pink insides. They were glossy. Juice oozed down to the top of her asshole. "Come taste me, lil' cuz. Get this pussy nice and wet before I let you fuck it in this nigga's palace. Come on." She slid a finger into herself, then sucked her juices off of it.

I climbed on to the bed and pushed her knees to her chest, licking up and down her crease before burrowing my nose into her hole, sniffing her up. I love the smell ofpussy.

She moaned and arched her back. "Uhh! Hell yeah, eat this pussy, lil' cuz, then come fuck me in his house. You hear me? Unnn-a." She pushed the back of my head, forcing me further into her crack where my tongue licked, before I sucked on her clit, nipping at it with my teeth. I was slurping up the cream that ran out of her in thick rivers. I could feel my chin already coated with it. "Awww! Yes! Eat this pussy, Jayden. Aww, my fucking God!" She screamed, thrashing her head from left to right, with her eyes closed tightly.

I took my two middle fingers and fucked her as hard as I could with them, while I sucked on her clit as if I was trying to pull it from her body. My tongue flicked at the groove of her pee-hole. Every time I went inside of it, she jerked and screamed at the top of her lungs, squirting more of her essence into my mouth. I started to go crazy; hitting her with every combination that I could think of. My fingers were a blur, and the noises I made between her legs were loud and nasty. She flopped around on the bed and tried to get away from me but I had her ass trapped and wasn't letting her go nowhere until she came in my mouth. I wanted to swallow that shit. I needed too.

"Jayden! Jayden, holy shit! Jayden, I'm finna cum on yo' tongue! I'm finna cum on your tongue, cousin! Awwwww-shit-yesss!" She screamed, throwing her head back, before cuming all over my mouth.

Even while she was shaking, I continued to suck that clit and flick it with my tongue. Her juices shot into my mouth over and over. They ran down my neck and on to my chest before I flipped her onto her stomach and licked up and down her ass crack, playing with her little hole back there. I was thinking I would welcome myself back to the A by fucking her big ass booty. Myeesha was definitely holding weight back there, and I wanted in. I sucked her clit from the back with my nose in her asshole. I pulled on each lip one at a time before sucking them both into my mouth.

She rose to her knees and pulled her cheeks apart, laying her face on the bed while she moaned deep within her throat loudly. "I swear I love you, Jayden. You so fucking nasty. I love you with all my heart! Uhhhh-fuck!"

I pulled on her clit with my teeth, then sucked it into my mouth, swallowing her nectar. She spread her knees wider and held her ass cheeks apart for me. I got on my knees and rubbed my dick head up and down her slimy slit, and got ready to slam it home when there was a pounding on the door. I slid in, pulling her back to me by the use of her hips.

"Uhhh-fuck yes! You're in me now, Jayden. Fuck me! Fuck me as hard as you can. I missed it so much!" She crashed into my lap with force. Looking back at me, she licked all over her lips.

I plunged deep into her womb again and again. Our skins smacked against one another. She felt tight and slippery at the same time. Her heat seared my penis and motivated me to go as hard as I could while the pounding on the door got louder.

"Uh, uh, uh, fuck! Who the fuck is it?" She screamed, picking her head up from the bed while slamming back into me on savage mode.

I sped up the pace and got to killing that pussy— digging deep into her, sending the bed into a rocking frenzy. Her ass jiggled every time it crashed into my stomach. There were light traces of sweat along the small of her back, and the way she had her ass in the air I could watch how her sex lips opened to accommodate me. It was a sight to see. "Gimme this shit, Myeesha. Word is bond." I growled, going full speed.

Her eyes rolled into the back of her head. She laid her face on the bed, picked it up and said, You killing me! You kiling me! Holy shit it feel so good!" She looked back at me, sucking on her bottom lip, then licked all over her lips again before laying her head back on to the bed, and screaming for me to cum in her. "Please come in me, Jayden. I wanna feel that forbidden shit, nigga! Please!" She screamed.

I smacked that ass one time real hard, and continued to work that pussy. I was trying not to focus on who was at the door, or if they'd left or what. I needed to cum deep within her pussy, or I wasn't going to be able to have a clear head around her. She was way too bad for that.

"Cum in me, Jayden. Aw shit. Cum in me. Here I cum, cuz. Awww, shiit!" She screamed, turning her face to the side on the bed with her eyes closed tightly. I felt her walls vibrating. Her pussy squeezed my dick again and again.

I watched my pipe fly in and out of her. Saw the way her juices coated my stalk when I pulled out, and the way her fat lips smashed inward when I slammed forward, and it became too much. I smacked that ass as hard as I could, one good time. She yelped and that's when I came deep within that pussy, popping my back until I was empty. Then I fell on top of that fat ass booty.

Myeesha clenched her teeth and rolled her ass in a slow circle. "Umm, that shit felt so good, Jayden. I'm so glad you're down here. These niggas can't fuck me like that. They're too intimidated to." She stretched her neck to kiss my lips, then flipped all the way on her back, pulling me on top of her.

I tongued her ass down while I played with that meaty pussy. "Who was that at the door?" I asked, sucking my fingers into my mouth.

She rubbed all over my chest and held her legs wide open while my dick rested in between her sex lips. "It was probably just Miah, or the maid. Either way, they don't want shit. Probably was just being nosey. I'll get to them when I get to 'em." She kissed my lips again, closing her eyes. "Thank you too, baby. I needed that." She got up and grabbed her gown off of the floor. Bending all the way over, she busted that pussy wide open for me with straight legs.

She peeked at me and smiled. "You glad you came down here now ain't you?"

I smacked that big ass and nodded. "Hell yeah."

* * *

Miah looked me up and down as she sat the box of Captain Crunch cereal on the table, beside the whole milk. "Dang, I can't believe that you're my cousin though. I barely remember you." She walked over to the cupboard, opened the cabinet, then stood on her tippy toes to reach into it so she could grab a bowl for her cereal.

I couldn't help peeping her on the low. She had on this black and white Fendi cheerleading outfit that was so short that it exposed all of her thighs and the bottoms of her ass from the back. She looked to be a few pounds heavier than Myeesha, and a shade darker. She reminded me of a caramel skinned Meagan Good, if Meagan Good had long, curly hair with a mole on her upper lip. She was also slightly bow legged with a southern drawl.

"We must got family all over the world fa real. These hoes about to be all over you. I'm telling you that now." She grabbed two bowls, closed the cabinet and handed me one.

"Good looking, lil' cuz." I took the bowl and sat it on the table and watched her pour her cereal into it. "Say, how old are you now?" I asked, curious. She was so bad that I was feeling guilty for peeping her the way that I was.

"I'll be eighteen in two weeks. I can't wait. I'm finna turn up and set this mansion on fire. Myeesha say I can work at her club then too. I'm trying to get my own money and take over the game. These hoes ain't ready for me. Believe that." She scratched her scalp, then poured milk over her cereal. "Why you ask me that? Be honest, too." She smiled knowingly.

I laughed. "Nah, I was just looking at how strapped you is, and I just wanted to make sure that you were grown, nah'mean?" I looked into her green eyes, then looked off. It was something about her lil' ass. I knew I was gon' have to be careful.

She giggled. "What? You already thinking you gon' be fucking me like you is Myeesha?" She took a spoonful of cereal and put it into her mouth, crunching loudly, looking me over closely.

Before I could respond, Myeesha walked into the kitchen with her car keys in her hand. "Come on, Jayden. Let's go and get you some clothed and shit. You gon' have to toss all that old shit you brought from Philly. It's a whole different swag down here in Atlanta, and we gotta make sure that these niggas ain't on yo' level. You feel me?" She grabbed her Gucci purse off of the counter. "I'll meet you out front in five minutes, so eat fast."

I nodded and watched her leave the kitchen. Seconds later, I heard the front door close, so I turned to Miah and smiled. "I can see that you gon' be a problem, huh? You think you 'bout that life or something, lil' cuz?"

She shook her head. "I don't know what you talking 'bout." She laughed. "All I'ma say is that you gon' find out what Atlanta all about. You ain't in Philly no more. The bitches run this shit down here. But you gotta have all of this." She stepped away from the counter, turned around and pulled her Fendi skirt upward, before twisting her hips, making her ass cheeks jiggle on each side of the thin strip of cloth that separated them. She looked over her shoulder at me and smiled, stood up, grabbed her cereal and walked off shaking her head.

I had to smack myself on the face to get that image out of my head. Like I said before, I could already see that Miah was going to be a problem.

That day, Myeesha took me to the mall and blessed me with a whole new wardrobe. She even made sure that I had a few pieces of jewelry to set everything off. When it was all said and done, I felt like I was ready for my new beginnings in the A. I didn't know all the things that this city would have in store, but it wouldn't take long before I found out.

Ghost

Chapter 5

I didn't meet Percy until a week later, after Myeesha rolled out to the airport and they came back home together. I knew I didn't like this nigga from the moment we locked eyes. He had one of them real cocky and arrogant demeanors about himself. I didn't like the way he looked me up and down as if I wasn't shit when Myeesha first introduced us in his kitchen, but I extended my hand anyway and shook his balmy one.

"Yo, it's nice to meet you, kid. I hear a lot of good things." I said, imagining myself blowing his head off while I looked into his eyes and smiled.

He was about 6'3" and was skinny with wavy hair. I could tell that he was mixed with something, because he was high yellow with gray eyes and freckles all over his face. "I always found it kind of funny that all you east coast niggas start y'all raps and sentences with saying yo." He laughed. "Why is that?" He looked me up and down with his upper lip curled. I wanted to bust him in his shit for asking that dumb ass question. Yeah, I didn't like this fuck nigga already. It was gon be hard for me to not bash his skull in.

I shrugged, making eye contact with Myeesha who looked at me pleadingly. "I don't know, kid. I guess it's just the culture, nah'mean? It is what it is. You south niggas got y'all own lingo too. Some of us find them funny, but we can't trip." I sucked my teeth and trailed my eyes up to him, feeling my temper rise.

He laughed. "Well, anyway, me and you need to have a sit down, so we can get an understanding amongst ourselves. I got some shit I wanna put on your brain. Shit that's gon' test your gansta right away. So why don't you go ahead and get yourself together, and we'll meet in my study in about two hours or so. How does that sound? In the meantime, I'll send Isabella to your room so she can give you a massage. She should be pulling up within the next ten minutes. That sound good?"

I nodded. "Yeah, that's a bet, bruh. I'll see you in a few."

He turned and smacked Myeesha on the ass so hard that she jumped. "You come up here and get me right. You already know what I need." He pulled her into his embrace and kissed all over her neck, squeezing her big booty that was encased inside of some tight Nine West jeans that left very little to the imagination. I don't know why, but seeing his bitch ass do that got me jealous as hell. I didn't want him touching her in my face. It was as simple as that.

Myeesha smiled, and looked into my eyes, then up to him, grabbing his right wrist. "Come on, baby. I already know what you need and I got you. Jayden, make sure you're on time so there is no discrepancies. My man works on punctuality, so that's how it has to go. Ain't that right, daddy?" She looked up at him.

He cuffed that ass and squeezed the cheek harder before looking over to me. "You see, Jayden, this how you gotta have shit. As bad as she is, she still submits to me. That's power. Any man that can get something as raw as her to submit, you know he must be the shit." He mugged me. "I gotta have her take care of me, then I'll get up with you. Two hours, be on time." They walked off with his arm around her lower waist.

I waited for them to disappear before I swung at the air four quick times, imagining that it was Percy's face.

Miah stepped into the kitchen shaking her head. "That nigga think he God or something just 'cause he got all that money." She sucked her teeth, walked to the refrigerator and pulled out a pitcher of pink lemonade, grabbed a glass out of the cupboard, and poured herself some. She looked me over closely. "What make it so bad is that he wouldn't have none of that money if his brother didn't leave it to their mother when he got indicted, or they didn't rip off those Fulton County Bloods. But he gon' get his. I'll just be glad when he does." She took another sip from her drink, still looking over the rim at me.

I tried to mentally process everything that she'd just said. I wanted to ask her questions, but felt like it'd be best if I kept my thoughts to myself. I'd figure things out on my own, I was sure of that. I walked over to her and held my arms open.

"Gimme a hug Miah." I looked into her green eyes, challenging her to deny me. I already saw that she was one of those real jazzy and stuck up types that liked to have men fawn all over her, but I wasn't going. I had a trick for all that shit.

She pursed her lips, smiled, and rolled her eyes before walking into my arms after putting her glass of lemonade on the counter. She wrapped her arms around me, hugged me, then looked up at me. "The only reason I'm giving you this hug right now is because I can tell you don't really like that nigga just like I don't. You was in here swinging at the air and shit. I found that funny, but I also get it. Trust me, the more you get to know him, the more you'll actually want to punch him in the face." She hugged me tighter, then looked up and kissed me on the cheek before walking away with her tight, Prada denim Daisy Duke shorts all in the crack of her ass.

I ain't gon' lie, I couldn't take my eyes off of it. I was trained on it until she left the kitchen. Miah had some type of way about herself. It was gon' be a task for me to stay away from her lil' bad ass, but I was going to try as hard as I could.

* * *

Percy placed a box of Cuban cigars in front of me after opening the top of them. He smiled, took one out and sniffed along its body. "Take you one of these, Jayden, and I promise it'll change your life." He said, looking down at me.

I took one of the cigars out of the box, sniffed it, and could already detect the strong scent of Ganja coming out of it. "Oh yeah? Why you say that?" I asked, sitting back in the leather seat, looking him over closely. I sniffed the cigar again and nodded. I was ready to put some fire to that big boy.

Percy curled his upper lip, sat the box on his desk, and closed it. "First of all, you gon' be the only muthafucka in Atlanta blowing this yellow shit. It's called Havana, because it's grown within the heart of Cuba. I get this shit straight from the source, so you should feel honored to be blowing this shit with me in the first place. Secondly, the fact that I am extending one of my Cubans to you is a sign of friendship and partnership. I heard that you were a savage back east. That you put the city on their heels and made them honor your gangsta. That's what's up because I got a few problems down here that I'm going to need your assistance with, and if you assist me, I'll make sure that it's well worth it. You can quote me on that." He took a lighter and lit the end of his Cuban before inhaling deeply, looking me over.

I was already puffing on my blunt, and after two hits my eyes were low and it sounded like there was a low-pitched hum in my ear. My heartbeats were thumping loudly, and my mouth was drier than a desert. I felt good. "Yo, I'm all about that paper, kid, so all you gotta do is let me know what it is, and what you're trying to accomplish. Word is bond." I took three more strong pulls and blew the smoke out of my nose, already lifted. That high made me feel like ol' Percy wasn't so bad.

Percy opened his desk drawer, took out two eleven by eight sized photos and slammed them on his desk. He mugged me, then picked one of them up and handed it across the desk to me. I took it and looked the photo over closely, scrunching my face.

The picture was of a skinny, dark skinned man with a mouthful of gold and long dreadlocks that stopped in the middle of his chest. I nodded and handed it back to him. "And? What you showing me this for?" I asked then pulled off of my blunt, inhaling and waiting for his response.

He licked his lips and curled his upper lip again. "I got fifty gees say you whack this nigga for me before the weekend is out, and this is light work, but it's a start. You show me how you get down by bodying this nigga, and I'll have a list of jobs lined up for you that will be more lucrative than this one. I'ma get you right." He leaned on the side of him and opened another drawer that was on his desk, went inside of it and came up with a bundle of cash with a rubber band wrapped around it. "This is twenty bands right here. Here. It's yours." He tossed it across the table to me, sat back and continued to puff on his Havana Loud.

I thumbed through the bundle of cash and nodded. "So who is this nigga?" I asked, setting the cash on his desk, then dumping the ashes from my cigar into the ashtray that was on his desk. I picked up the picture again, studying it closer.

"He's an enemy. That's all you gotta know, and I got fifty gees that say you fuck him over, while I watch of course. I forgot to add that part." He sucked his teeth and rocked in his chair.

I shrugged. "Aiight, so, you should know that I ain't that familiar with this city, so I'm gon' need a location of where I can find him, and how to get there. Long as you can provide me with all of that, you can consider this nigga dead and have my other thirty gees, nah'mean?" I ran my tongue over my teeth. For some reason, they felt as if they were getting numb. I started to wonder what fuck that Havana was all about.

Percy smiled and nodded. "Oh, you don't worry about the location and all that other shit. I just need for you to study that picture as best you can, then go ahead and get fitted for the night because we'll be stepping out for a few hours. I hope you like the

Seventy Sixers because they're playing our Hawks tonight, and I think we should be present." He smiled. "You ever sat on the floor of an NBA game before?"

I continued to mug the picture that was in my hands. I didn't know what the fuck he was talking about and how that was relevant so I decided to ignore it. "How soon can I handle this business and where do you wanna be when I do it?"

He licked his lips and rocked in his chair. "Aw, you gon' handle this shit tonight. After taking that twenty gees right there, you now officially work for me. Everything is going to be on a need-to-know basis. Believe that."

I picked up the twenty bands in cash, thumbed through it, then curled my lip and threw it into his chest. "Nigga, fuck this chump change. You ain't gon' be talking to me like I'm one of these weak ass niggas from down here. I'm from Philly, son, and I'm a fucking god, nah'mean? If we gon' do business, the first rule you gon' follow is that you gon' respect me and my mind, or shit ain't gon' fare to well for you. Feel me?" I said, standing up and stubbing out my blunt in the ashtray. This nigga had my heart beating fast as hell. I didn't like no man acting like I was his bitch or something. That bowing down shit wasn't in me at all. I would've rather knocked Percy's head off and took that final thirty than to let him come at me sideways.

He sucked his teeth and looked up at me with a deathly stare. "You finished?" He continued to puff on his cigar with a mug on his freckled face.

Just hearing him ask me that question caused my temper to rise to the point I was seconds away from exploding. "What?"

He held up a hand and closed his eyes, shaking his head. "Look, Jayden, I ain't trying to disrespect you, homeboy. I just feel like you being on a need-to-know basis will help you down the line. Now my ear have been to the streets of Philly. I know how you get down, and I'm the only nigga in the A that do. That's a benefit for me and you. Now by you being in the streets and getting down the way that you did back east, I know you had to come across all types of different killas and mobs in the ghetto. My only fear is that you find out who you're going to be knocking off and it'll make you feel some type of way, or it'll lead back to a connect that you had back in Philly."

I shook my head. "Nah, son, don't think for me. You just tell me the target and his history to you, 'cause he ain't got none with me. Far as what I feel, I don't feel shit for no man, that includes you. My cousin in love with you. I don't give a fuck about you or no other nigga. Let's get that shit straight. However, I'm about my paper. So, any nigga you talking you want me want me to hit, for the right price I'll knock his fucking head off. Point-blank, period. If we gon' do business, you need to know that I ain't one of these fuck niggas that you used to dealin' with. You keep that at the forefront of your mind and allow me to think for myself, we'll be good."

He nodded. "You know what? I can respect all that. Let's start over and go from there. Aiight?"

I mugged him for a long time, then sat back in the leather chair. "Yeah, that's cool. Now who is this nigga, and why do you want him bodied?"

Percy sucked on his bottom lip, looked over my shoulder, got up and walked around his desk and closed his office door. Then, he cleared his throat as he paced the floor in front of me. He took a deep breath and blew it out. "His name is Kano, and he is second in command for the Fulton County Bloods. These niggas are lethal, and ever since my brother been gone, Kano been demanding that I pay him twenty thousand a week out of each of the four of my strip clubs. That's eighty gees." He shook his head. "My brother Gino was a Blood from East Atlanta. These niggas used to run the streets and hustle together. They even dropped a few hot tracks in the studio back in the day that had the city on fire, but they wound up falling off over a bitch. The same bitch that had something to do with my brother getting indicted. Long story short, now that my brother is out of the picture for the next fifty years, I guess Kano think I'm fair game, and since the city saying that my brother Gino is working with the Feds so that he can get out on his appeal, I'm getting shunned by Georgia right now. I'm fair game, and this fool Kano is making it his business to capitalize off of that fact as much as him and his crew can. I can't continue to afford to pay him eighty gees a week, so he gotta go. It's as simple as that." He walked back around his desk and sat down. "Now, tonight is his sixteen-year-old son's birthday. The lil' boy is a Seventy Sixers fan. I sent them a pair of floor seats for the game, so I know that he's going to be there with him, which is why we're going, and I'ma have you trunk his ass, and bring him to the dungeon where you will torture and kill him in front of me. The better the job, the bigger the bonus. Now, how do you feel about that?" He asked as he wiped his mouth with his fingers. He gave me a look that said he was worried.

I picked up the picture from his desk again and smiled. "Shit, far as I'm concerned, this nigga is as good as dead." I nodded. "Let me go and get fitted. It's gon' feel good seeing the team from the homeland."

Percy bent over, picked up the $20,000 in cash, and handed it across the table to me. "This right here is a token of my appreciation. It ain't got nothing to do with the fifty thousand that I'm going to pay you for this move. You hear me?" He stood up and extended his hand.

I took the money, looked down at his hand, and balled my fingers into a fist, giving him dap. I didn't like touching other dude's hands and shit. I didn't see any purpose in that. "We good, bruh. I'll see you in a lil' while."

* * *

I was just fitting my left foot into my gray and black Retro 8 Jordan's when Miah came into the room. She looked over her shoulder then closed the bedroom door behind her. Walking over to me with her finger held up against her lips. "Shh, Jayden." She looked over her shoulder again.

She then went to the stereo system in my room and turned on a song from Gucci Mane. Afterward, she walked swiftly back to me, pulling downward on my neck. "Jayden, I didn't mean to be eavesdropping. Well, I guess I kinda did, but anyway, that doesn't matter. I couldn't help but to overhear you guys' entire conversation, and the first thing I wanna say is that I love yo' ass, because I can see that you're a gangsta, whereas Percy is a pussy. Anyway, that dude Kano is major. Most of the Bloods in Atlanta fall under him and they pledge their allegiance to him and Capo, and Dream.

"Now Percy wants you to knock him off, which I understand that because they keep their foot in his ass, but it's worth way more than fifty K. After you hit Kano, the city of Atlanta is going to be set on fire, because The Fulton County Bloods are already beefing with the ones from East Atlanta. That was Gino's crew. It's a bunch of politics that goes along with it. But long story short, you're killing a major dude, and it will not end there. Percy is too stupid to see that. All I ask is that you are careful because I really want to get to know you the way that Myeesha does." She leaned forward and kissed me on the cheek then walked out of the room, taking one last glance over her shoulder, before leaving and closing the door behind her.

I took the picture of Kano from under my pillow once again, and looked it over. I could already see what kind of a man I was dealing with when it came to Percy. He was a coward. One of those that was afraid to get his hands dirty. Instead, he'd rather pay protection fees, and for real killas to do his dirty work for him. Luckily I had a cousin like Miah who was hip to all of his bullshit and was there to put me up on game. I knew what I had to do, and nothing would stop me from doing exactly that.

Chapter 6

I watched Embiid take the basketball, cock it back and dunk it with so much force that he left the rim rocking. It caused the arena to quiet down, but I had a big ass smile on my face. I felt like a part of Philly was in the building with me, and even though it made me feel homesick, I was thankful none the less to see the ballers from my homeland.

Percy tapped me on the shoulder, then handed me the pair of high-powered binoculars before leaning with his lips on my ear. "If you look directly across the court, you'll see that nigga and his punk ass son sitting with them bright ass red Gucci fits on. You can't miss 'em." Then, he took a nacho chip and tossed it into his mouth, smacking in my ear.

I looked over at him and pushed him away, wiping my ear and mugging his stupid ass. "Damn, nigga, back yo' yellow ass up." I said, irritated.

He laughed under his Ray Bans,and sat back in his chair, nodding with his head over to Kano and his seed. I placed the binoculars up to my eyes, and looked across at the pair just as the ten basketball players that were on the floor ran past my lens to the other side of the court. Kano picked up his cup of beer, took a sip out of it, and sat it back down on the floor, before pulling out his cellphone and texting away on it. I trailed my gaze over to his son, and saw the boy pumping his fist in the air as Atlanta scored a three pointer. He hopped out of his seat and waved a red Gucci towel around his head. He was dressed up like one of the Migos, and I noted he had a bunch of gold chains around his neck, with diamonds sparkling on them.

I took the binoculars away from my face and handed them back to Percy. "Yeah, I see 'em, kid. What about it?" I picked up my Sprite and drank from the straw.

He shook his head. "Just wanted you to see how that nigga looks in the physical; that's all." He tossed another chip into his mouth, and crunched down hard on it before picking up his beer and drinking half the cup.

"Yo, you already know that I ain't one of them average niggas, right?" I said this just as two of the players on the court got into a shoving match. The referees ran over to break them apart, giving both players a technical foul.

Percy pulled his nose and sniffed loudly. "I thought we already talked about all that." He said, looking out on to the basketball court. I watched him screw his face up and pull his nose again.

I sucked my teeth. "Well, the streets say that nigga Kano got pull over majority of the Bloods in the city. The streets say that after I knock him off, it's a guarantee that a war is going to jump off. What you got to say about that?" I asked, leaning close enough so only he could hear me.

He shrugged. "The streets ain't paying you seventy thousand dollars to whack his bitch ass, I am. So, until the streets do that, fuck 'em." He sucked his teeth and pulled on his nose again. I could tell that he tooted some form of dope because that was a classic habit of tooters.

A part of me wanted to check this nigga for saying fuck my source, but I had to keep in mind that he didn't know that my source was Miah. He was just playing the tough role. I had to let him have that because I already had plans for his ass down the road. I nodded. "You right. I'ma handle this nigga, and I'll meet you at the spot you showed me." I looked across the court at Kano, then his son before finishing my Sprite and leaving my seat.

* * *

I could feel my heart pounding in my chest. My mouth was dry, and I couldn't stop the palms of my hands from sweating underneath the leather gloves that I wore over them. The air was incredibly thick, and it was hot and humid as fuck as I laid on my back with my eyes wide open, trying to breathe through my mouth because I was tired of smelling the heavy scent of gasoline underneath Kano's car. I'd already stabbed his left front tire, causing it to deflate before I slid under it and awaited his presence. I had a brand-new .45 in my hand cocked back, ready to shoot. The ski mask on my face had me sweating like one of the basketball players from the game.

I must've been under there for at least thirty minutes when I started to hear crowds of people all around, talking loudly about the game and saying how much the Hawks sucked that night. People got to loading into their cars and pulling out of the their parking spaces before entering the heavy line of traffic that led out of Phillips arena.

I swallowed, when ten minutes later, I heard the sound of footsteps getting closer to Kano's red BMW. I saw the shoes of him and his son on each side of the car, before the driver's door was opened, the lock was popped, then his son opened the passenger's door and got in, talking a mile a minute. Soon both doors were slammed, and the car's engine turned over. Kano stepped on the gas a few times, started to back it up, then slammed on the brakes.

He put the car back in drive and pulled it back into the parking space before getting out and walking to the front of his whip. "Aw, hell n'all, man. How the fuck this happen?" He asked. He kneeled in front of the tire and looked it over closely, stood up, reached into the whip and popped the trunk. I watched his shoes travel across the concrete, all the way to the back of the car.

The passenger's door opened, and his son stepped out. "What's good, pops?" he asked with only one foot on the concrete.

"I got a flat. I probably drove over some glass or something. It ain't no big thang. I'ma handle this business, then we up out of here. Get back in and sit back." He ordered.

I swallowed once again and tried to hold my breath because the fumes from the exhaust were killing me. I felt like I was getting lightheaded and I didn't know how much more of that I could take as I watched him roll the spare tire across the concrete, stopping at the front of the car.

I laid as still as possible. I watched him raise the car with his lifter, then he took off the old wheel, and replaced it with the new tire, grunting and making all kinds of noises as if he were struggling to do the job. After five minutes of all the sound effects, he tightened the last bolt, then stood up, and rolled the old tire across the concrete toward the trunk. I waited until I saw him lift it up to place it inside of it, before I rolled from underneath his car and crouched.

A majority of the cars were out of the lot, and the few that were left looked to be about a hundred yards in front of us, waiting in line before they could enter into the traffic that was heading away from Phillips arena. Kano got ready to close the trunk and must've remembered the jack, because he swore to himself and then made his way around to the front of the car where it laid by the front left tire. As soon as he took a step to his left, he saw me, and his eyes got as big as paper plates.

I put my finger to my mask where my lips would have been, and shook my head, motioning for him to come toward me while I aimed the .45 up at him.

He looked all around the parking lot as if he were looking for someone to help him, or for a place to run. I didn't really know which, and I didn't care. If I had to, I was going to gun his ass down right there, put a hole in his son's head, and keep it moving. Lucky for me, he nodded and slowly walked toward me with his hands in the air in front of his chest.

As soon as he was close enough I stood up, and slammed the pistol under his chin. "Greetings, bitch nigga. Let's get yo' punk ass in the car before I knock yo' head off. Feel me?" I said balling his shirt into my fist. "Open that backdoor."

"Say, Mane, you don't know who you robbing, homeboy. I suggest you do your research before you pull yo' capers. This ain't gon' end well." He said, trying to look back at me.

I muffed him with force. "Bitch nigga, open the door and get yo' punk ass in before I wet yo' son." I lowered my head to look into the car and saw that his son had the passenger's seat all the way back and appeared to be knocked out. I smiled. It seemed like everything was falling into my favor for the most part.

Kano opened the backdoor and started to get inside of it. As soon as he bent down, I turned the pistol around, cocked back and slammed the handle into the back of his head, right above his neck and below the skull, knocking him out cold. He fell onto his stomach, and that's when I took the zip ties and placed them on his wrists that I'd pulled behind his back, and pulled on the slack until they were tight around his wrists. Then, I pushed his ass on the floor and popped the trunk of his car, pulled out the tire that he'd placed in there and threw it on the ground, before going into his whip, and loading his ass into the back of it. I looked around the parking lot and everything seemed to be in order. Before closing the trunk, I crept around to the passenger's side and looked into the window. Sure enough, there was his son, sleeping like he'd worked all day long.

I pulled open the door and pressed the barrel of my .45 to his cheek. "Wake yo' bitch ass up and get in this trunk, lil' nigga!" I hollered.

He jumped and his glasses fell off of his nose and on to his chest. "Wait, what? Aw, shit! Pops! Pops! Aw, man, what's this about?" His eyes were wide open. The side of his face was glistening with slobber on it.

I grabbed him by his Gucci shirt and yanked him out of the car, making him walk in front of me. "Get yo' lil' ass in the trunk next to yo' old man before I cap you."

"Aiight, man, aiight. Just chill. You ain't gotta do all that, homey." He slowly climbed into the trunk with his back to me.

I waited until he had both feet inside of the trunk before I swung the gun with full force and crashed it into the back of his head, the same place I'd hit his father. He fell on his chest and was snoring before I closed the trunk back.

* * *

Kano struggled against his binds with a frown. Beside him, his son cried tears of panic while he struggled very little against the duct tape that had him bound to the chair in Percy's dungeon.

Percy stepped over to him, stripped the tape away from his face with a big smile. "Look at yo' punk ass now. Where is all them Blood niggas when you need 'em, am I right?" He laughed and adjusted the glove on his left hand.

Kano spit a loogey at him and tried to break through the duct tape. "You bitch ass nigga, you know it ain't sweet. You come at me like this. Got my lil' one all involved. You dead muthafucka. I swear you better kill me!" He growled before once again struggling to break free of his binds.

Percy nodded at me, and I picked up the Louisville Slugger that he'd given me before we came down to the dungeon. I tightened my hand around the base and wound it a few times before placing it on my shoulder.

Percy smiled and looked down at Kano. "You ain't tough, Kano. You just got a bunch of dumb niggas that follow behind yo' soft ass. You know that, and I know that. But to prove to you that you ain't tough, I'ma make yo' bitch ass cry." He nodded at me again. "Fuck that lil' nigga over, homeboy."

I stepped in front of Kano's son, cocked the bat back, and swung it forward as hard as I could, connecting with the side of his head, feeling the wooden bat vibrate in my hands. *Bam!* The bat broke the skin immediately. Blood popped into the air. Kano's son jerked in his seat before falling backward, and then forward with his head laying in his lap. A thick line of blood oozed out of the open wound.

"Noooo! What the fuck!" Kano hollered with his eyes bugged out of his head. He struggled against the binds. "Awwwww, I'ma kill you fuck niggas!"

The dungeon felt hot and sticky. It looked like a huge basement, though it had nothing in it but a bunch of armed chairs that I guessed were used for the purpose that we were using then in that moment. The floor was all concrete, and the walls were padded to muffle the sounds that took place down there.

Kano's son tried to pick his head up while thick globs of blood poured out of his wound and ran down his neck, saturating his Gucci shirt. "Dad, why is this happening?" He said breathlessly. His eyes rolled into the back of his head.

Percy frowned, walked over to him and smacked him so hard that it echoed in the basement. "Wake yo' ass up. I can't enjoy this shit if you sleep." He went into his pocket and pulled out a tablet of some kind and broke it under Kano's son's nose, causing the boy to jerk awake with his eyes wide and alert. This made Percy laugh. "Yeah, that's what I'm talking about."

"Arrrghhhh! This ain't got shit to do with my baby. This about yo' snitching ass brother. He don't have to be doing what he doing. He could take that time like a man. Let's leave the kids out of this." He looked over to his son and I saw his eyes become glossy.

Percy shook his head. "N'all, nigga, it's about you hitting my pockets and pulling rank over me. I don't give a fuck what my brother do. That's between you Blood niggas. But when you fucking with my bread, you gotta pay the cost. Bash his lil' one shit in, homey, and don't stop until that lil' nigga is dead." Percy stood back, and I stepped forward with the bat already over my head.

I took a deep breath and brought it down over the boy's skull with so much force, busting his shit wide open. Then I swung the bat from the side and created another hole, swung again and created another, and another, and another, until I was going crazy while doing my thing to him. In my mind, I was killing Nico all over again. I had to mentally detach myself from the situation, because if I took time out to think about the fact that I was bodying a kid, I wouldn't have been able to do it, so I had to play mind games with myself.

The entire time Kano begged for me to stop. "You killing my baby. You killing my baby. Aww, shit!" He kept on saying again nd again, until his son's chair flipped over and he laid on his side with his head bashed in.

I took a step behind Percy with my chest heaving. I glanced at the boy one last time, saw how I'd left him, and felt a bit of remorse before shaking it off. I knew that night I would have a hard time sleeping, but it was a small price to pay in the grand scheme of things.

Kano lowered his head with tears rolling down his cheeks. "You a bitch ass nigga, Percy, I swear to God. I should've killed yo' punk ass when I had the chance. Something told me to." He shook his head. "You ain't gon' get away with this. On my Blood, you ain't gon' get away with this, nigga. Karma is a bitch!"

Percy held out one hand. "Let me see that bat, Mane."

"Kill me, nigga. On my son, you better kill me, or I'm coming for you and that grimy ass mixed bitch of yours!"

I felt offended as soon as the words left his mouth. I swung and punched him directly in the jaw. "Watch yo' mouth, nigga. That's my cousin." I moved out of the way.

"Fuck that bitch. She gon' reap what she sewed. She gon'—"

Percy side-armed the bat and connected it with Kano's jaw, knocking his head sideways before winding back and swinging it again, connecting it with the back of his head. Blood spurted out of him and across the padded walls. He groaned in pain.

Percy handed me the bat. "Kill this nigga, then load the bodies into the back of that pickup truck upstairs. I'll show you where we gon' take 'em." He said, taking a step back and wiping his hands on his shirt with a disgusted look on his face.

"I got you, kid. Fuck this nigga." I swung the bat and connected with the back of Kano's head again, then proceeded to beat him senseless with no remorse. All it took for me to carry out his murder was for me to continue to replay the things that he'd said about Myeesha, over and over again in my head.

Ghost

Chapter 7

"This here is a Bentley Continental with a hard drop, and got more horse power than the Kentucky Derby. I laced it with the all-white leather Gucci seats to set off the black on black custom paint job. When the sun hit yo' shit, you'll be able to see the Gucci logo inside of it. I put four screens in it for you. One in each of your hear rests, one in the dash, and a five-inch inside of your driver's side sun visor. This bitch sitting on twenty-eight inches of solid gold. Look in that passenger seat right there. You see that? Check that book bag because everything inside of it belongs to you." Percy said, shielding his eyes from the sun.

It was so hot that I felt like I was about to die. I couldn't keep my tongue inside of my mouth. I was missing that Philly weather already. Atlanta felt like I was always in the microwave being cooked to death. We were in the driveway of Percy's big mansion, and I was walking around and appraising the new Bentley that he'd copped for me as a token of his friendship. Even though I didn't I give a fuck about that nigga, and in my mind we were the furthest from friends, I wasn't turning down my collar to a busting ass whip like the one that sat before me. I opened the passenger's door and pulled out the book bag, opened it and saw that it was full of cash. I smiled at that and nodded at him.

"Well, what do you say, Jayden? You think you can become my right hand man and we can take over this city the way that we're supposed to?" He asked, sipping out of a bottle of Ace of Spades.

I tossed the book bag on to the seat, walked around and sat behind the wheel. It had only been ten days since I'd bodied Kano and his son, and if this was the thanks I got for doing something as small as that, then I could only imagine what was to come. I stood back up and hollered over the hood of my new whip. "Yo, how much money is in that book bag?"

He laughed and held up his bottle. "I thought you'd wanna take the joy to count it and find out."

I shook my head. "Hell n'all, it's too hot for all that. Give me a number." The sun beamed down on my forehead, cooking me alive. I could feel my upper lip perspire.

He waved me off. "It's chump change, Mane. Just a hunnit and fifty thousand. You know, weekend spending money. You keep fucking with me, and you gon' see that on a regular." He raised his bottle again then drank out of it.

Miah walked out of the house wearing a pair of tiny white Fendi shorts that had her thighs jiggling with every step that she took. She also wore a belly shirt that showcased her flat stomach, with the pink diamond in her belly button. She walked over to the car and ran her hand across it. "Damn, this boy is lit right here. You definitely finna take me for a drive in this bad boy." She licked her juicy lips and popped back on her legs, shielding her eyes from the sun so she could look up at me.

My eyes were on Percy, and his were all over her rounded ass. I mean, he was eating that boy up. I even saw him shake his head. "Damn, as soon as the Queen of Spades open up, I'mma make sure you run that bitch, Miah."

She looked over her shoulder at him and licked her lips again. "Long as you talking the right numbers, then we good. I told you I already got offers from Onyx, the Dollhouse, and the Cheetah Lounge, and they're all talking advances. They willing to make an exception for me. What are you willing to do?" She rubbed her stomach then played with the pink diamond in her belly button.

Before he could respond, Myeesha walked out of the front door with a pitcher of pink lemonade. She had on a short, light Eves St. Laurent summer dress, with her long, curly hair pulled back into a ponytail. I kept on forgetting how bad she was because Miah had me lowkey feeling some type of way. "Y'all thirsty out here?" She looked from Percy to me.

Miah shook her head. "He might be, but me and Jayden finna roll out so y'all can have the palace to yourselves. Come on, Jayden. Take me for a spin in your new whip. I wanna show you the city anyway." She walked around the car and got into the passenger's seat, closing the door, and started to mess with the controls on the digital dash.

I shrugged as I made eye contact with Myeesha. "I guess lil' cuz wanna rollout, so we'll see y'all a lil' later."

Percy lowered his eyes. "That's cool, but I want you to fuck with me tonight, Jayden. I got some shit I wanna run by you. Maybe we'll make a night of it."

I nodded. "Yeah, aiight, that sound cool." I sat in the driver's seat and closed my door, before pulling away from Percy's mansion, feeling good that I was going to be able to spend some time with Miah.

* * *

We'd been rolling around the city for a full hour, just cruising and taking in the sights when Miah took a deep breath, reached over and touched my right hand, catching me by surprise. I looked over at her curiously. "What's good, lil' cuz?"

She looked into my eyes and smiled. "So what's your deal, Jayden? I mean, what brings you down here to Atlanta of all places?" She took a strand of her curly hair and put it behind her left ear, then began to play with the diamond in her belly button while looking me over closely.

"I came down here to get a fresh start. Plus, it's plenty money down here too. Philly burnt up for the moment, so I needed a change of scenery and a change of pace. That's about it."

She sucked on her bottom lip and scrunched her eyebrows. "But aren't you the reason it's burnt up?" She laughed. "Myeesha said that you're a goon and that you fucked over a lot of real killas before you left Philly. She said that you were deadly. That's a quote." She licked her lips, looking into my eyes.

"Myeesha might be exaggerating a lil' bit. You know how the family do. But, nah, I ain't taking no shit from nobody. I'm a Philly nigga and we are how we are, nah'mean?" I made a left and rolled past Lenox Square Mall out in Buck Head. It was only a few miles away from Percy's mansion.

"Yeah, well Myeesha could be putting a lil' extra on you, but I don't think she is, 'cause she wasn't saying that shit to me. She was trying to convince Percy of that long before you came down here. I don't know what they're up to, but you better be careful. I see you already handled your business with Kano. I mean, he been missing for a lil' while now so I can only imagine he wound up on that receiving end." She smiled and looked out of her window.

As soon as her head was turned, I couldn't help but to notice that she was rubbing on her right thigh unconsciously. Her short shorts were all up in her crack, leaving both thick thighs exposed. I damn near rolled up on a curb I was peeping her so closely, and feeling bad at the same time.

She looked over to me and bit into her bottom lip. "You know I can see how you peeping me from the reflection of the window right?" She laughed and shook her head again.

"Yo, you gotta put all that shit away or something. I can't focus on what I'm supposed to be doing with them thighs out like that. I got a problem." I made another right, and sped up the pace on the Bentley. "Far as what you talking about with Kano, you gotta stay in yo' own lane and don't assume nothing. It's best for you to chase your dreams than to be trying to keep your ear to the streets, or dibble and dabble in the slums, nah'mean? Besides, don't you have some goals that you want to accomplish in life?" I looked over to her, then back to the road.

She sighed out loud. "I don't really know anymore. I used to think I wanted to be a doctor of some sort when I was little. Then I wanted to be a lawyer, but as I got older I started to realize that all those things were far-fetched and I didn't want to be either one of them at all. I had only said them 'cuz it's what every other kid was saying around that time. What I wanna be now is a top-notch stripper. I wanna hit niggas' pockets and make men bow down to me.

I hate how us women are objectified and treated like shit everywhere we go, or anytime we try and rise out of the gutter. Nothing makes me happier than breaking a nigga down, and leaving his ass feening and in need for me, then I shit on they ass." She curled her lip and frowned. "I hate Atlanta, Jayden. These dudes down here ain't right. You'll see that. Especially Percy." She lowered her head. "I can't wait to break out of this city. If you was to ask me what my dream is, that's my dream." She took a deep breath and adjusted her seatbelt. "Make a left up here and follow this road for a mile. I wanna take you somewhere and show you somethin'."

I nodded and followed her directions before looking over at her. "Say, Miah, I can tell that you really don't fuck with that nigga Percy, and you just made it seem like it goes deeper than what I can imagine, so what's good with that fool? He ever put his hands on you or something?" I glanced back over to her.

She fidgeted nervously in her seat and took a deep breath before blowing it out. "Look, Jayden, I don't want to get into all that because I see how you get down. The smartest thing for you to do right now is to handle whatever business that Myeesha got you down here for. She knows what's up, and one thing I know about my sister is that she always gets the last laugh." She smiled and pointed. "Pull up to that gate right there so I can get out and put the code in."

I slowly pulled up to the intercom that was on the side of the big metal gate that was blocking us from entering into the gated community that was before us. "Yo, Miah, before you get out and do all that, I just want you to know that I love you, lil' cuz, and I'll fuck a nigga's whole family over for you. Don't think you ever gotta hide shit from me, you feel me?"

She smiled, looked into my eyes and nodded. "I feel you, Jayden, and thank you for saying that. It means a lot. Trust and believe me when I tell you that." She squeezed my hand, then got out of the car, walked up to the big intercom and punched in a digital code. At once the big gate began to slide to the left, then she got back into the whip, and ran her fingers through her long, curly hair. "Drop the top on this Bent, so you can make a statement when you pull up. We going down this road, and you gon' make a left at the end of this street and pull into the second big driveway that you see." She pulled out her phone and got to texting on it.

Once again, I followed her directive. I hit the button for the hard top to remove itself, and fold into the trunk in such a way. As soon as it disappeared, the sun made its presence known, beaming down on the both of us and heating up my leather seats almost immediately. I looked over to Miah again and saw that she was applying her Kylie Jenner lip gloss.

"Jayden, when you get up here, I want you to bring all that Philly swag out. Make these bitches feel some type of way because I got plans for them, and these plans involve you, whether you know it or not." She looked into the mirror on her makeup case, puckered her lips, then put it all back into her Fendi purse.

"Yo, I'm just gon' be me. I don't change for nobody, and we gon' have to discuss what you talking about a lil' later on too."

She smiled and pointed at a red bricked mansion where I could see the front door open and two brown skinned females come out of it. "Of course we will, but for now, just turn on that Philly shit. My hustle depends on it."

* * *

I took a sip of the lemonade then pulled off of the Garcia Vega that was stuffed with Kush, inhaling deeply while the wind blew so hard that it caused the Vega to burn wrong. Kenya— a brown skinned female who stood 5'6" with brown eyes and a body of a goddess— walked up to the table I was sitting at that had an umbrella over the top of it to protect me from the sun, stopped in front of me and looked into my eyes. She had on this two-piece Marc Jacobs bikini that looked like it was two sizes two small. The panties portion was magnifying her sex lips, and her D cup titties were damn near falling out of her top. She'd just gotten out of the pool that was in front of me, and her body was dripping wet and glistening. She looked good as hell and was strapped. I looked her up and down and gave her my approval of being a bad chick. I even peeped her toes that were perfectly pedicured and had a French tip.

She licked her lips. "So, I hear you from Philly," she said with a hand on her hip. She popped back on her thick legs and batted her eyelashes at me.

I nodded. "Yeah, that's the land. Why? What's good with it?"

She smiled. "Nothing. I just like east coast niggas. Y'all got a different type of swag that's different from dudes in the A. Wish our boys were more like y'all."

Miah walked over beside her and smiled, lowering her eyes at me. "My cousin ain't just the average Philly nigga though, Kenya. He got mad respect out there. They call him a Street King, and he got niggas that roll under him. When we open our club to compete with all these other ratchet ones in the A, he's going to make sure that we have top-notch security, and all those ballers come through from out east. He fuck with Meek and all of them. Ain't that right, Jayden?" She looked into my eyes and bucked hers as if to say I better go along with her story.

I exhaled my weed smoke and nodded. "I love my lil' cousin, so whatever she want, she get. Word is bond."

Kenya licked her lips, turned to Miah, grabbed her and kissed her lips, rubbing all over her ass while moaning into her mouth. She reached between them and unbuttoned Miah's shorts, and pulled them all the way down her thighs, allowing for her to step out of them. "I love her too, Jayden. She owns me, and I'll do anything that she says." She looked up at Miah while squatting so she could rub the front of her panties.

Miah spread her legs and licked her juicy lips. By the way that Kenya was squatting, it caused her G string to go all the way into her crack. Her ass cheeks were busted open for my view. Miah pulled her up, and once again they began to tongue each other down. Behind them, the other female looked on from the pool, holding a big beach ball in her hand with a big smile on her face. They moaned. Miah's hands were all over Kenya's ass, rubbing and separating the cheeks while she sucked on her neck.

"Jayden, I want you to fuck this bitch so she can know that this shit ain't a game. Show her how you get down. Give her that Philly dick." She slid her hand into Kenya's panties and began to rub in between her sex lips, while Kenya stood on her tippy toes, moaning at the top of her lungs in the big backyard.

"You gotta watch though, Miah. I'm not letting no man touch me unless you're watching." She moaned, leaned in and they were making out again, loudly.

Miah squatted and pulled Kenya's bikini all the way down, exposing her bald pussy. She grabbed a handful of her hair and forced her to bend over the table on front of me. "You see how I treat this bitch, Jayden? I don't coddle these hoes. This bitch father got all this money from fucking with them movies out here in Atlanta, and I'm gon' have Kenya get us every penny that we'll need in order to open our club. Ain't that right, Kenya?" She smacked her on the ass and pulled on her hair so that her head snapped backward.

"I'll do whatever you say, Miah. Just let him fuck me and talk that east coast stuff to me while you watch. That's going to be so hot." She moaned and spread her legs widely.

Chapter 8

Miah slid two fingers into her from the back, and worked them in and out of her while Kellis sucked all on Miah's neck and licked her ear lobe. I didn't notice how strapped Kellis was until that moment, because her ass was right in my face, poked out and swallowing her Burberry G string.

I pushed the table to the side and sat my chair right in front of Kenya, before she unbuttoned my shorts and fished my hard dick out. She stroked it, running her tongue over her lips. Because Miah had her bent over, she had to rest her left hand on my thigh, while her right one pumped my stalk.

"Suck his dick, Kenya. Let me see you get him off." Miah moaned, with Kellis sliding her hand up her shirt, massaging and playing with her titties. She eyed my dick and never took her eyes off of it. "Unnn, hurry up, Kenya, I wanna see it."

Kenya sucked the head into her mouth, swallowing half of the pole before bringing her lips back up to the top, only to suck it again.

"Damn, Jayden, you got a big dick. I can't wait to see you fuck my friend with that." Miah said, turning around to face Kellis.

They sucked on each other's lips, then Kellis dropped and pulled Miah's panties down her thick thighs and off of her ankles. Miah bent over just enough for her pussy to pop out. I could see both bald lips peeking at me from between her thick thighs.

My dick jumped in Kenya's mouth. She moaned around it and sucked me harder and faster, while I guided her head and watched Kellis open Maih's pussy lips. She slid two fingers up her hole, working them in and out of her. It seemed like every time she pushed them into her and pulled them back out, they would be coated with more and more of her juices, to the point that Miah's juices were running down the back of her hand and dripping off of her wrist.

"Uh, uh, ooo-a, yes. Play with my pussy just like that." She moaned before looking over her shoulder at me with her eyes glazed over.

Kenya sucked me harder and harder as Miah and I locked eyes. Then I trailed mine down to her pussy, where Kellis was fingering her so hard that Miah's thighs were shaking.

Kenya reached into her bra and pulled out a Magnum, tore it open with her teeth, put it into her mouth, and slid it down my pole in one motion. "Now I wanna ride you while you watch my sister eat Miah out. Make sure you turn to where he can see, Miah. Oooh, this shit so hot." She straddled my lap, holding on to my dick, and slowly guided it into her dripping wet pussy while I held on to that fat ass booty. As soon as my head slid through her lips, I felt her heat searing me. "Uhh!" She moaned, leaning her face into my neck. "Fuck me, Jayden. Fuck this pussy!"

I grabbed her ass, made her rise, then slammed her down on my dick. Picked her up, and slammed her down again, and kept on repeating the process. Her cat was nice and tight.

"Uh, uh, uh, uh, ummm, ummm, ummm, uh, uh, oooo-a, shit, uhh! His dick is huge. It's so fucking big!" She screamed.

Miah walked over to the table and sat her bare ass on it, while she rested her left hand on my shoulder, spreading her legs wide. Kellis kissed her lips, then stuck her face into Miah's pussy. I could hear the slurping sounds, and watched her finger her at full speed. Miah moaned at the top of her lungs and ran her hand all over my chest. "Uhhh, this bitch a beast. This bitch is a beast! Uhh, fuck, it feel so good!" She threw her head back and grabbed a hold of her titties through her belly shirt, pulled it all the way up to expose them, and I watched her pull on her erect nipples, rolling them between her thumb and forefinger.

I stood up, taking Kenya along with me, and bent her over right beside Miah, slid back into her pussy and got to fucking her from the back like a maniac as I watched Kellis play with and eat Miah's pussy. I could smell the scent of it, and it drove me crazy. Kellis would open her sex lips, exposing Miah's pinkness, before she stuffed it with two fingers and ran them in and out of her while she sucked on her clit.

"Uhhh! Shit! Fuck me! He killing me, Miah! Yo' cousin killing me! It feel so good! Harder, harder, Jayden! Uhhhh, shit!" She screamed, slamming back into me and cuming all over my dick, while I kept my eyes trained on Miah's fat pussy. Miah squeezed her titties together, ran her hand down her flat stomach, looking me in the eyes. She blew a kiss at me, then flicked her tongue and ran it across her lips before giving me the *come here* sign with her forefinger.

I was digging deep into Kenya. I was fucking her so hard that my dick was a blur as it drove in and out of her tight pussy. She screamed underneath me and begged me to go harder, throwing her ass back into my lap. I watched it ripple while juices oozed out of her and slid down her thick thighs. I leaned forward, and Miah grabbed the back of my head, causing me to slow down a lil' bit. Then, she was sucking all over my lips before darting her tongue into my mouth. Her titties rubbed against my chin. I could feel the hard nipples poking at me, so after we broke our kiss, I latched my lips around it, then licked it.

"Uhhh, Jayden, you're too much. You're too much!" She hollered as she arched her back and came all over Kellis' munching face, while she rubbed all over my lips with her finger.

Seeing her sex faces pushed me over the edge. I gripped Kenya's hips tighter, and slammed into her again and again, beating her her walls loose. She started to scream so loud that it sounded like I was killing her, and I probably was trying to. *Bam, bam, bam, bam, bam!* Harder and harder I went until I felt my body tingling all over. I started to jerk, and slammed into her again before I was cuming over and over, with her slamming back into me, milking my pipe.

"He's cuming! He's cuming! Uhhh-shit, I feel his dick jumping!" Kenya hollered.

Miah ran her tongue all over her lips, pinching her clit, looking into my eyes. "Now, both of y'all suck his dick. I just wanna watch." Miah moaned, pushing Kellis' head away from her and toward me.

Kellis dropped as if she were Miah's robot, just as I pulled out of Kenya with her juices all over my condom. As soon as my dick was out, Kellis sucked my dick into her mouth, then pulled the rubber off of it, licking all over the head, smacking her lips loudly. "Yeah, he taste good. I can suck his dick all day long if you wanted me to, Miah." She licked my head and sucked me deep into her mouth.

Miah slid two fingers into herself, driving them in and out while she looked down at her. "Kenya, get yo' ass down there and suck my cousin dick too. I ain't gon' tell yo' ass again."

Kenya tried to balance herself on wobbly legs. She looked exhausted. Her hair was all over the place, and sweat slid down the side of her face, on to her neck. "Okay, Miah. I'm sorry." She whined, kneeling and sucking my head into her mouth while Kellis held it out for her.

Then, the next thing I knew, they were taking turns sucking me and stroking my dick while I watched Miah finger herself, and play with her nipples.

She'd smashed her sex lips together, then open them real wide, exposing her little hole, digging deep within herself, before pulling them out and rubbing them all over my lips and nose. "You smell me, Jayden, huh? Tell me what I taste like." She moaned, sliding her fingers into my mouth.

I sucked them and licked all over them hungrily. Her scent was intoxicating. She was making it hard to stay away from her lil' ass, 'cause believe when I say I was seconds away from snatching her up and bending her over like I'd done Kenya.

Kellis ran my head all over her face and looked up at me. "Can you cum over both of our faces, Jayden? Please? Just do it, and let Miah watch." She stroked my dick faster and faster while Kenya licked up my thigh. She reached into Kellis' panties and started to finger her at full speed.

Miah leaned over and grabbed the back of my head again, sucking on my lips, sliding her tongue into my mouth, while I played with her titties. "I'ma let you fuck me on my birthday, Jayden. You gon' be the first man to hit this pussy, I promise." She moaned, licked all over my neck, then put her nipple on my lips.

That was all I could take. As soon as my lips wrapped around her nipple, I started to cum in thick globs all over Kellis and Kenya. They took turns sucking the nut out of me, then they placed my head between their lips and started to kiss my head at the same time. In the process, they were making out with each other. The only thing I kept thinking was, "Welcome to Atlanta!"

* * *

On the drive home, Miah couldn't stop looking over at me and smiling. "Did you enjoy yourself, Jayden?" She licked her thick lips then laughed a little.

I nodded. "Yeah. Why them broads follow you like that though? What you got on them and be honest?" I made a right at the light and stepped on the gas, headed back to Percy's mansion so I could shower and get some sleep for a few hours.

She laughed and shook her head. "I ain't got nothing on them, and I don't need anything 'cause I'm up here, Jayden." She pointed to her temple. "When it come to bad bitches like them— ones that have a lot of money and that have pretty much had the world sat before their pretty toes— it takes a female like me to fuck their head up, and feed something that they're not used to." She picked up the bottled water from the console, twisted the top, and took a long swallow before replacing it. "Females are more emotional than physical. It is easy to conquer a woman if you feed her emotions. Once a woman's emotions are fed, you can pretty much get her to do anything physical. You see, with Kenya and Kellis, their parents are never home. They are always on the road, making business moves to further their family's prestige and income which is understandable. However, what they have failed to realize is that they have two daughters, and both girls are very emotional and mentally vulnerable because since birth they have been raised by either a nanny, or a house keeper. To compensate for the lost time, all their parents do is shower them with money and gifts. They never take the time to feed their children where they are the most poor, which is their mental and emotional state of mind. Long story short, ever since we were in the first grade, I've been the one filling those voids for them. Their father has become major in the movie world, and it's time I capitalize off of both girls financially. They know what it is, and they gotta make it happen one way or the other. It's as simple as that." She wiped the corner of her mouth with a finger and looked over at me. "You kinda see where I'm coming from?"

I nodded. "You're a beast, lil' cuz, and it's blowing my mind the way your brain works. I gotta honor it though, because you just out here figuring it out like the next go getter. I see you can't be taken lightly either because you are a thinker, just like me." I looked her over and nodded. "Yeah, I like that."

She smiled and squeezed my hand. "Jayden, what I said back there about you having your homeys from back east hold us down on the security tip when our club opens, can that really become the truth? I mean, would you be willing to do that?"

I nodded. "Yo, I got you, lil' mama. Whatever you need. I thought you was only bullshitting. So, you ain't finna fuck with the Queen of Spades when they open it up?"

She shook her head. "Hell n'all. I want bitches to dance in my club, not the other way around. I was born to be a boss, not an employee." She shook her head again. "That shit ain't for me. I can't have no man sit back and clock dollars off of me while I only get a percentage. I can't see it. So, yeah, I keep my sister and her nigga guessing, thinking I'm gon' be a dependent forever, when in all actuality I'm busting the right moves and pulling strategic strings. I want it all, and I'ma get it. You'll see."

We pulled up to Percy's mansion after going through the process of having the gate opened down the road. I parked behind his Range Rover and turned off the ignition, looking up at his palace, knowing that one day soon I was gon' have one of my own.

Miah leaned all the way over, slid her hand in my lap, and cuffed my dick, squeezing it in her small hand, looking me in the eye. "You're a real nigga,

Jayden. You got that killa shit in you that people only see in the movies. I like you, and I want you to fuck with me on that level. I meant what I said about my birthday. I want you to fuck me like a grown ass man. Don't take it easy on me neither because I gotta learn." She kissed me on the cheek, then put my hand between her thick thighs. Miah unbuttoned her shorts, opening her legs wide to slide my hand into her panties. "Unnn, shit. You feel that?"

Her sex lips felt meaty and hot. There was still juices along the lips from her playing around with Kellis. My finger bumped against her erect clit. "Hell yeah, you real hot down there." I said, feeling my dick get hard.

She spread her legs wider and forced my finger into her hole. Her lips closed around the digit. "Unnn. Whenever I give you this pussy, Jayden, I want you to cherish it because I never thought I'd let a nigga fuck me until I met a savage like you. If I'm gon' give some of this body up, it gotta be to a money-making, cold-hearted goon. I don't like soft or broke niggas." She pulled my fingers out of her box and placed them on my lips.

Just like before, I tried to suck the skin off of my fingers while I feasted on her essence. "Yo, you got that killa shit in you too, lil' cuz. I wish I could have found a female that thought and got down like you do. I'da probably married her ass a long time ago." I joked but was kind a serious too.

My lil' cousin had mad swag. I was jocking that shit to the utmost. I didn't know where she'd gotten it from, but it appealed to me. I truly loved her and wanted to help her accomplish all that she had in mind.

She opened the door to my Bentley. "Well, if she was like me, she wouldn't let no nigga put a ring on her finger and tie her down. She'd get her own jewelry and find other ways to conquer his ass. Women run the world, Jayden. Trust me on this. I love you, cuz, and we gon' do it big for my birthday." She got out of the car and closed the door behind her.

I watched her switch her hips all the way until she got to the front door and went inside. Everything that she'd said replayed over and over in my head, and on top of that, I still couldn't believe how bad and advanced she was. I shook my head and made my way inside.

Chapter 9

Percy slid a .45 automatic with a silencer under the table to me, picked up the bottle of Moet, and smiled as the heavy-set, dark skinned man by the name of Dream stepped into our VIP section of the Dollhouse strip club. He had a bunch of gold links around his neck. He wore all black Burberry pants with the matching button up, and around his waist was an all red Ferragamo belt. They matched his red shoes. He snapped his fingers and the two Brazilian strippers that were casually dancing to the music in front of our table nearly broke their necks to get out of the room. As soon as they were gone, two of his goons stepped into the room and closed the door, as Rae Sremmurd's "Power Glide" began to bass out of the speakers in the club. I looked past his goons and saw the strippers going wild behind them.

Dream smiled a mouth full of gold and red diamonds. "What's good, Percy? Seem like it's nearly impossible for me to book a meeting with yo' ass. Luckily I got eyes and ears everywhere, so when you booked this room for the night, my associates got back to me and let me know you'd be here. May I sit?" He asked, opening the palm of his hand and pointing to a seat across from Percy.

It was the same seat I'd just witnessed the two Brazilian girls making out with one another on. There was still a strand of one of their hairs on the back of the red leather couch.

Percy puffed on his Cuban cigar and nodded at the spot. "Be my guest." He looked over to me and lowered his eyes.

I picked up the bottle of Ace of Spades and turned it up. I swallowed it in big gulps while I kept the .45 positioned on my lap. I didn't really know what Percy had in mind, but I knew that Dream was Kano's right hand man, so I was ready to start busting if it came down to that.

Dream sat down and pulled out a small Ziploc full of all kinds of pills. "I got Mollies, Peres, Oxy's, and Methadone. What you niggas want?" He asked looking from Percy to me.

Percy put up a hand and shook his head, and I ain't even acknowledge this nigga. I knew I'd killed his right hand man, so I didn't like him. I was dead set on treating him like it was all his fault. Fuck him.

He snapped his fingers about a foot away from my face. "Hey you, did you hear me? What you deaf or something?" He asked looking me up and down.

I trailed my eyes over to him and curled my upper lip. Then, I picked up the bottle of Ace and drank from it again. "I'm good, homey. Keep yo' hands on your side of the table though. My hearing is fine." I sat the bottle down and looked into his red, murky eyes. I could see the sweat glistening along his forehead.

He smiled and grunted. "Oh, is that right?" He looked over to Percy. "Who is this nigga?"

Percy puffed on his cigar and blew a cloud of smoke to the ceiling, before taking the cigar out of his mouth. "That's my family from out of town. He gon' be down here for a minute."

Dream nodded. "Well, clearly this nigga don't know who I am, or who this city belongs to."

I shook my head. "Nope, and I don't give a fuck either. But it's obvious you don't know who I am, and what I mean to *my* city." I mugged him with hatred and tightened my hand around the handle of my pistol, ready to fill him with holes.

He frowned and sat closer to the table. "Where the fuck you from, Blood?" I noticed his goons that were behind him stick their hands in their suitcases, right along their sides.

I sized them up real fast and decided that I would shoot at the one closest to me first, then put holes in the one that was further away, before I knocked Dream's head off of his shoulder if it came down to it. "I'm from Philly, nigga. Born and bred." I sucked my teeth, still looking him directly in the eyes. I was numb after tooting a few grams of Percocet.

He frowned and leaned forward a little closer. "You bang red or blue? Let's nip this shit in the bud right now."

I shook my head. "Neither. I bang for that green. That's it, that's all."

He looked into my eyes for a long time and nodded just as three police officers walked past our VIP section and to the front of the club after glancing our way. "Yeah, aiight, Blood. I'ma give you a past for right now, at least until Twelve come out of this muhfucka. In the meantime, I'd advise you put yo family up on game, Percy. That way he just might be able to make it out of the A." He mugged me and sat back in his seat, while his goons eyed me with anger.

I pulled on my nose, sniffed loudly, and turned the bottle of Ace back up, swallowing while looking at him.

Percy laughed. "I'll do just that. But I know you ain't tracked me down so we could discuss a man that you didn't even know was here until today. What's on your mind, Dream?"

Dream popped two red pills, chewed them up, then chased them with the bottle of Moet that was on the table. "That fool Kano been missing for almost ten days now. I wanted to know if you heard anything. I know you keep your ear to the streets."

Percy shrugged. "Nah, I ain't seen nor heard from him for a lil' while now. I'll see what I can find out if you want me to." He said puffing on his cigar, while holding it between his teeth.

Dream nodded and looked up at his goons. "Yeah, well I got a tip that says you're lying. A lil' bug say you bought him two tickets for the game, in honor of his son's birthday. Coincidentally, the cameras from the game shows him and my lil' homey being stuffed into his trunk before the person that did it drove off with them. Now every nigga in the A know what it is with us Fulton County niggas, and don't nobody want that heat. It leads me to believe that you had to have something to do with it, being that you a shiesty nigga and all."

I cocked the hammer on my .45 and felt my heart beats pounding in my chest.

Percy looked into Dream's eyes and smiled. "You got something you trying to say without saying it, Dream?"

Dream slammed his hand on the table, knocking over the ashtray. "Kano was supposed to pick up sixty gees from you every week to fund our Blood niggas, which means that you and him would've had to make contact within the last ten days. Not only that, it means that you would've had motive to knock my nigga off. All I wanna know is if you did it."

Percy shook his head slowly. "Nah, I ain't touch Kano. We had an understanding. There was no bad blood there."

"Yeah, well, fuck nigga, I feel like you lying, and since my nigga ain't here to collect, how about you run that sixty bands to me, and we can keep this protection thang going, or else."

I shook my head. "N'all, kid, he pay me for protection now. You fuck boys ain't got shit else coming. Word is bond." I said, eyeing him closely with my gun pointed at him under the table.

He jerked his neck backward and bugged his eyes out of his head. "Mane, you better tell this nigga to stay in his place, Percy. I ain't gon' warn you again."

I turned my head to the side and glared at him. "Nigga, I don't give a fuck about yo' threats. You don't run me, kid. Word is bond. Like I said, I'm from Philly, nigga. You don't hold no jurisdiction over the god. I said he pay me for protection now. That's just that."

The lights started to flash off and on in the club as one of their feature dancers took the main stage and got to doing her thing. The MC announced who she was and invited all patrons to crowd the stage and make it rain for her to insure that she'd be back at a later date.

Dream's goon stepped forward and looked like they had bullshit on their minds.

I extended my arm, put the barrel of my .45 to Dream's chin, and stood up. "Bitch nigga, you better tell them fuck boys to get on they knees and place their guns on the table. I got a silencer on this muhfucka which means that I'll knock yo' head off, and won't give two fucks about it. Like I said, I'm from Philly, nigga. Fuck you, and fuck them. Now give the order. Now!" I forced it firmer into his skin.

"Put y'all guns on the table man and kneel. Hurry up!" He ordered, sounding like a bitch to me.

His goons took their pistols out of their holsters and placed them on the table, before putting their hands in the air and kneeling.

"Grab these niggas' pistols, Percy, and put them on your waist. Dream, you coming with me, nigga. Stand yo' punk ass up." I walked around the table and jammed the pistol into his side hard enough to break one of his ribs, leading him out of the VIP room, and into the back hallway where the bathrooms were, while the club continued to go crazy over the dancer on stage.

The lights flashed on and off, and the stage lit up bright green. I poked Dream's ribs harder and forced him to walk all the way to the back, where the exit sign was. Once there, I pushed him through the door and out into the back alley where Percy had parked his Benz truck. Usually there would have been two security guards at this exit, but Percy had already paid them off, which was a good thing because the way I was feeling, had I gotten any hassles from anybody, I would have wasted them with no hesitation.

"You fucking with the wrong nigga, Mane. I don't know what Percy thinking but you are committing suicide, homeboy. This ain't Philly."

I took him by the back of his neck and drove his face into the side of Percy's truck like a mad man. He fell to one knee and I kneed him in the ribs.

He hollered out in pain.

"Bitch ass nigga, I told you I don't give a fuck who you is. I am Philly!" I smacked him in the face with the pistol, splitting the side of his head open. His blood gushed out of him, just as Percy came out of the back door leading Dream's goons at gunpoint. I slammed the handle into the back of Dream's head, and watched him fall to the pavement. "You bitch niggas see this shit? Huh? This the nigga you calling Capo, huh?" I raised my gun, aimed it at one of them and fired, sending a bullet into his shoulder, knocking a chunk of meat from him.

"Awww shit!" He fell to the ground with blood gushing between his fingers. I loved hitting niggas in their shoulders. It always made them pay attention, and after the wound healed, they'd never be the same.

The other goon's eyes got big. He tossed his hands up. "Say, Mane, don't shoot me, Blood. I ain't got no beef with you." He looked from Percy to me, and I could see his knees knocking together. I almost laughed at that.

Percy came and stood behind me while I held him at gunpoint.

"Listen, nigga, I want you to go back and tell your niggas that it's a new sheriff in town. N'all. Matter of fact, tell them that Philly is here and we taking over Fulton whether they like it or not. Tell them that Dream is my bitch, and I'm taking his slot. If they wanna get money, then fuck with me. If they

wanna die, then that can happen too. Word is bond."
I turned the nigga around and searched him until I
uncovered his wallet. I took out his ID and put it in
my pocket. "You go to the law, I'm bodying yo'
whole family, kid. Keep your ear to the street and
listen for how I'm going to do this nigga right here.
Run, nigga, go!"

He slowly backed away with his hands up,
looking me in the eye the whole time. I guess when
he felt comfortable enough, he finally took off
running at full speed down the alley, never looking
over his shoulder.

I opened Percy's backdoor and loaded Dream's
big ass into the backseat, while Percy got behind the
wheel. Before he drove off, I got back out of the truck
and shot the other goon twice in the chest, then
jumped back into the truck as Percy sped away from
the scene.

* * *

Blood dripped from the corner of Dream's mouth,
onto the concrete floor of the dungeon. He coughed
and swallowed. Both of his eyes were black, and one
of them was barely open. I'd watched Percy do a
number on him. He swallowed. "We was supposed
to have a truce, Percy. Me and Gino straightened out
our differences. You gon' start a whole new war with
this shit," he said out of breath.

Percy kneeled and laughed, puffing on another
cigar. "I don't give a fuck about no war, homeboy.
This is about money."

Dream took a deep breath and blinked the only
eye that could open. "Nigga, fuck that sixty stacks.

You can keep that shit. Just let me go about my business and leave my family out of this."

I swung and punched him so hard in the jaw that I almost fell. He fell out of the chair, onto his side. "Nigga, I told you about giving orders. I'm in control now." I grabbed a handful of his dreads and helped him back to the chair.

He started to cough and spit blood on the concrete, wheezing as if he had asthma or something. "Aiight, Blood, aiight. I get it." He lowered his head while his chest heaved.

Percy laughed and shook his head. "I gotta have the Onyx, my nigga. Sign these papers and make this shit official, then I want you to verbally state it for the record. Do this, and I'll let yo' bitch and kids live." He walked over to his open briefcase and came back with a bunch papers, handing Dream the pen for him to sign them.

Dream continued to wheeze as he placed his signature on each line that Percy pointed to. After he finished doing that, Percy took his phone and placed it up against Dream's lips. "I, Marshall Johnson, of sound mind and body, do sign over my club to Percy Morgart after being paid one hundred and fifty thousand dollars of legal US monies. I am not being coerced, or forced to do so. This deal became official on this day of August the thirteenth, of the year twenty eighteen." He said, reading the paper that Percy was holding in front of his face. "Aiight, man, now let me go. We can squash all this bullshit."

I laughed and shook my head. "Aw hell n'all. Nigga, you see, you gon' love the next part, because that's the part where I chop yo' bitch ass up, and spread your body parts all around Fulton County to show yo' niggas this shit ain't a game. Philly is here."

Percy walked over and handed me a Machete and stood back. "I always get the last laugh, Dream. It's been that way ever since I was a kid, and it's always gon' be that way." He looked up to me. "End this fuck nigga so we can put his parts on ice."

And that's just what I did. I took my time and cut that nigga up piece by piece, until he was nothing more than a torso. Percy took his limbs and placed them in one of his suitcases. Then, we poured gasoline all over his torso and burned it into ashes inside of a big metal garbage can that was in the back of his dungeon. Each one of Dream's limbs were bagged and placed in the deep freezer that Percy had upstairs from his dungeon.

It seemed like the longer I stayed in Atlanta, the crazier I became.

Chapter 10

I took the $20,000 in one hundred-dollar bills and threw them in the air so they could rain over Miah, while she danced in front of me with her diamond crown on her head. She was dressed in a Vera Wang mini dress with the matching red bottomed heels. The dress fit snugly on her body, showcasing all of her natural curves that caused me to feel some type of way. She moved her hips to the Cardi B track with her eyes closed, obviously having a good, with her arms in the air. We were in Percy's pool house after we'd partied with all of her friends to celebrate her eighteenth birthday. The only ones that were left were Kenya and Kellis. They blew their party horns and cheered her on while she danced in a circle.

"Yeah, Happy Birthday, Miah! Welcome to adulthood!" Kenya yelled before blowing her horn again.

I smiled. "That's twenty gees for you, baby girl. Happy birthday, ma." I stood up and gave her a hug. I tried to pull away, but she grabbed my head and kissed my lips, grinding into my front.

"We about to do it big tonight, Jayden. I want you to fuck me like you never fucked no bitch before. Can you do that, baby?"

I reached around her waist and grabbed a hold of that big ass, massaging the cheeks, causing it to rise a little bit. She moaned into my mouth. "Yo, if that's what you really want, then I ain't got no problem giving it to you, but I'm letting you know right now that I ain't gon' take it easy on you. You give me this body then I'm 'bout to go in. Word is bond."

She leaned in, looking me in the eyes, and sucked on my bottom lip. "I wouldn't have it no other way. Let's get it." She raised her head and nodded at Kenya.

Kenya got up and slowly walked over to the back of the pool house where she stopped in front of a light switch. She dimmed the lights until there was an eerie glow coming off of the pool that was shining in front of us. Miah walked over to the radio and switched the song to SZA's "The Weekend."

Then, she walked back over to me and stood on her tippy toes, kissing my lips. "I want you, Jayden. I been wanting you every since I caught you peeping my lil' frame when you first got in from Philly. So, take me, and show me how you get down." She grabbed my hand and guided me to the bed where we stopped, so Kenya and Kellis could finish decorating it with the red and white rose petals.

They looked over at us and smiled, then continued their task until they were done. After they finished, they came around to the side of the bed that Miah was on, and gave her a hug, and ended with pecking her on the lips, then they were gone.

Miah stepped on the bed, looked down at me, and started to dance to the song bellowing out of the speakers while she looked me in the eyes. She kicked her Red Bottoms off, wiggled her hips, slipping one shoulder strap off of her shoulder at a time until the dress fell around her pretty feet, then she kicked it on the floor and stood before me in some see-through, white Victoria's Secret panties that matched her top. I could see that the top was molded to her sex lips. The panties sank in between them and she had an exposed lip on each side. She ran her hands down her stomach and into her panties, spreading her legs, then sliding a finger deep into her center. She closed her eyes and moaned deep within her throat. The sight was almost too sexy for me to contain myself. I couldn't believe how bad this girl was.

After slipping her fingers out of her panties, she slid two fingers into her mouth and sucked her juices off of them. "I taste so good, Jayden, but you about to find that out though. I hope you wear my lil' ass out. I need that savage part of you." She pinched her nipples through her bra, then pulled on them, causing them to stand straight up against the material. The darkness of her areolas could be seen plain as day.

I took my shirt off and threw it to the floor before climbing on the bed naked from the waist up. Once there, I grabbed her lil' ass, picked her up and fell to the mattress with her, landing right between her thick thighs that wrapped around my waist.

She tried to push me off of her. "Nall, I changed my mind, Jayden. I don't wanna do this no more." She groaned.

I leaned down and sucked on her neck, licking along the thick vein on the side of it. I grabbed her chin and tilted her head back to give me better access, before biting into her skin and sucking on it with aggression. "I don't give a fuck what you want. I'm finna take this pussy. Who gon' stop me?" I asked, reaching between us and feeling all over her sex lips that poked out of her panties. I could feel that she was damp down there. I pulled the panties up some more, forcing the material to go further into her crease.

Then, I pinched on each lip, feeling their thickness while my thumb located her erect clit, flicking it .

"Unnn-shit, cuz. Fa real, let me up. I don't wanna do this. Umm, fuck, Jayden." She moaned and opened her legs wider.

I pulled the crotch band to the side and rubbed in between her sex lips, feeling how wet her pussy was. Its juices oozed out of her and leaked into her ass. I took a finger and found her little hole, rubbing all around it in short circles before sliding it deep into her body.

"Unnn! Shit, Jayden. Why you playing with me? Why you playin' with me, Jayden? Fuck me like a savage or get the fuck off of me. I ain't playing." She humped into my hand and ran her nails across my lower back.

I grabbed the crotch band once again, but this time I pulled on it and ripped her panties from her body in one yank.

"Uh! Shit! You gon' take this pussy or what? What are you waiting on?" She smacked me across the face, then pulled me down by my neck, kissing all over my lips while her thighs opened as wide as they could go.

I pushed her up off of me, took the backs of her knees and pushed them toward her chest, busting her pussy wide open, and then my face disappeared between her legs. I slurped her pussy lips into my mouth loudly, and slid my tongue into her womb, flicking it in and out of her at full speed. She tasted like strawberries mixed with a hint of salt. The scent of her pussy wafted up my nose, and the only thing I kept thinking was that I was about to fuck the shit out her lil' thick ass. I couldn't wait to get into that pussy; I ain't gon' even lie. I opened her pussy lips wide and watched her clit pop out from the top of her hood before I sucked on it like a nipple.

She bucked off of the bed, sat all the way up and fell backward. "Uh! Shit, Jayden! Oh my God! Uhhh!" She screamed and twisted her head, grabbing her own titties, pulling on her nipples through her bra.

I licked up and down her crease, sucked on her clit and nipped at it with my teeth, while two fingers ran in and out of her pussy. I needed to taste her cum in my mouth. I was curious to know how she tasted when she got off. "Let me taste that shit, Miah. Let cuz taste it. Come on, baby." I growled and went right back to work sucking on her clit so hard that I was pulling it an inch from her hood, while my fingers continued to go in and out of her. Her bald pussy lips were glistening with her sheen. They were fully engorged, and I licked all over them.

"I'm 'bout to cum, Jayden. I'm 'bout to come on your tongue, cuz. Uhhh-shit! Shit-cuz!" She opened her legs wider, then threw her head back against the bed with her hips bucking up into my mouth again and again.

I was sucking on her clit, trying to drain it of its juices, while my fingers attacked her nonstop. Her pussy skeeted into my face and I kept on swallowing; drinking her nectar, and loving every bit of it until she collapsed with her chest heaving.

I got on to my knees, grabbed a handful of her hair, and put my dick head on her lips. "Here, cuz. Suck this muhfucka. Hurry up so I can hit that pussy.

Word is bond." I ripped her bra off of her and gripped her right breast in my hand.

She sucked my head into her mouth, licked up and down the hole, then swallowed my whole pipe, gagged, pulled it out, and swallowed it again before I pulled it back out and got between her thick thighs. I noted that her pussy was wide open. The brown lips were puckered. I could see her shiny pink insides.

I ran my dick head up and down her crease while I looked into her green eyes. "You sho' you want this dick, lil' cuz? Tell me what you want for your birthday. I need to hear that shit again. Tell me!" I ran my head in circled around her protruding clitoris.

She raised up and muffed my face. "Fuck you, nigga. I ain't telling you shit. If you want this pussy, you gon' have to take it. Get the fuck off of me!" She pushed my chest and tried to wiggle out of my grasp.

I dug my nails into the back of her thighs and slammed my dick home with anger, breaking through her hymen. I felt it tear, and then her pussy got real wet. So wet that it began to pour out of her. "Hell yeah!" I hollered, cocked back and got to fucking her like an animal. My waist crashed into her pelvis again and again. I watched her bald pussy lips open and close around my dick, and the sight of it drove me crazy. I still couldn't believe that I was the first to get that pussy, but it was way too tight to not be the truth.

"Uh, uh, uh, uh, uh, Jayden! Uh, it hurts! Slow down! Oooh, fuck! Please! Slow! Down! Uhh, shit, it feels so! Oooo-a!" She moaned with her mouth wide open and her tongue licking all over her juicy lips and chin.

I leaned down and kissed her lips, and then we were French kissing while my hips slammed into her. I made sure I was long-stroking that pussy with no mercy. Hitting rock bottom, pulling back and slamming it home again.

She dug her nails into my back, licked all over my neck and bucked her hips into me. "Fuck me, cuz! Fuck me! Harder, cuz! Ooh, kill this pussy. Kill it! Kill it! Fuck me harder! Harder! Ooh, shit, I'm cuming!" She covered her face with her hands and screamed at the top of her lungs. "Un, uh, uhhhhh-shiit! He killing me!"

I sped up the pace and really got to digging into her pussy while she shook like crazy up under me. Her walls vibrated, and her cat seemed to try and suck me deeper into her before I aggressively flipped her onto her stomach, got behind her, raised her right leg and slid back in while I bit her on the back of her neck. That fat ass botty was in my lap now. Its meaty cheeks jiggled while I attacked her again and again with anger and lust.

"This my pussy, Miah. You hear me? This. Is. My muthafuckin'. Pussy. From. Here. On. Out." I fucked her like she owed me something, feeling my cum rise from deep within me. "Awww, this shit so good." There was a puddle of her juices up under us. Miah had that A-1 cat. I knew I was gon' stay in her body.

"Uhhh, fuck me, Jayden. Ooh, cuz, fuck me. Fuck this pussy. Ooh, shit, I love you! I love you so much!" She screamed as she came all over again, bouncing into my lap.

I grabbed a handful of her hair and pulled her unto all fours. I slid back into her, and got to fucking her so hard that I was hurting my abs. I clenched my teeth and gave her all that I had. Her pussy sucked at me and spat its juices all over my pole, while she laid her head on the bed, taking everything that I had to offer like a champion with tears rolling out of her eyes. I grabbed her hips for more leverage and gave her another seven bangs before I was cumming deep within her pussy in large spurts. "Aw, aw, aw, uhh-fuck." I groaned, skeeting into that wet ass pussy.

She pulled all the way forward so that my dick plopped out of her, turned around and sucked him into her mouth, deep-throating it while looking into my eyes with tears dripping off of her chin. "I love this dick, cuz," she said, popping me out of her mouth. "I love this dick so, so much." She rubbed it all over her face, licked the head and stroked it while looking up at me. My dick was still rock hard because of how bad she was. She looked into my eyes with her electric green ones and sniffed my head. "We ain't done, cuz. I wanna run the whole gambit. You been looking at this fat ass ever since you got here. Now I want you to do something about it." She sucked my dick back into her mouth and bobbed her head up and down on it for another two minutes before reaching under the bed and coming up with a bottle of KY lubricant. She squirted some inside her small hand, reached around her back and pulled her left ass cheek away from the other one so she could put the oil along her crease. Below, her pussy lips were wide open and looked as if they were breathing. I started to play with them while she got herself ready for me to fuck that ass. As soon as she finished, she looked over her shoulder at me. "Fuck this ass, big cuz. No mercy status. Like you say, word is bond." She laid her face back onto the bed and spread her thick thighs, looking back at me.

I kissed all over her cheeks, then bit them one at a time before rubbing her oozing pussy while I lined my dick head up with her tight asshole. I situated myself, then slowly moved inside of her while she played with her throbbing clitoris.

"Unn, unnn. Slow. Slow, cuz. Ooh, awww-fuck. Okay, it's in. Now do me like you been wanting to. Please, Jayden." She moaned, licking her lips again.

I slammed forward, holding on to her hips, sinking as deep as I could, then I got to wearing that ass out.

"Mmm, mmm, mmm, mmm, uhh-shit, mmm, mmm, mmm, uhhh, ooh, you, fucking me, cuz. It's. So. Deep. Ooh, it's so deep!" She hollered.

Faster and faster, and as hard as I could go, I pounded that ass out and broke her in the right way. Her heat seared me, and the snug was so tight that I knew I wasn't about to last too much longer. The sight of her playing with her clit while I fucked her, the way her ass jiggled every time I crashed into it, her nipples rubbing against the bed sheets, and her moans became too much. I had to cum, so I got to beating that asshole open at full speed, growling like a bear. "Urrr, urrr, urr! Here. I. Come. Lil' cuz, here I come. Uhhh-fuck!" I hollered and came deep within that ass, just as she started to scream at the top of her lungs while her fingers worked magic on her vagina's nipple.

* * *

Afterward, she laid on her back while I held her small feet in my hands, kissing on each individual toe. They were so perfect that I had to worship them. Every time I saw her walking around in the house with bare feet, I peeped them boys, and I had to give her her props. A female that kept her toes done was my weakness. Miah not only had some good ass pussy and the ass to match, but she was a top-notch lil' chick, and I dug her swag to the utmost.

She smiled and wiped a bead of sweat from her forehead, looking up at me. "Damn, cuz, I'm surprised you ain't got a whole stable of bitches that followed you from Philly. Especially if you get down like this. You's a goon for real. I just wanted to let you know." She shook her head. "Stop kissing my toes and shit and come down here and hold me for a minute. Even though I really ain't the lovey-dovey type, I feel like you fucked it up out of me. C'mere." She sat up and held her arms open for me.

I slid between them and my dick laid right up against her pussy lips. I kissed her, turned my head to the side and sucked on her neck. I could taste the salt that was there. "Aww, so now you need me to hold yo' lil' tough ass?" I joked, laying on my back and pulling her on top of me.

She nodded. "Yeah, yeah, yeah, you got a bitch real emotional right now. Enjoy it, 'cause this don't happen too often." She closed her eyes and kissed my lips again. "Jayden, we gotta get our paper right. I got some shit up my sleeve that I wanna do, but I know it ain't right, so I need you to speak that killa shit into me, so I can go through with it." She sighed. "Can you do that?" She rubbed my cheek and looked into my eyes. It was the most vulnerable that I had ever seen her.

I nodded. "Shorty, whenever it come to surviving in the slums, you going to always be faced with moral type decisions, but more often than not you ain't gon' have no choice but to overlook that shit and keep it moving. Besides the money, don't shit else matter. So, you gotta do what you gotta do, 'cause that's exactly what I do. Ain't no room for remorse in this game ma. Word is bond." I kissed her lips.

She continued to rub my face after we broke our kiss, looking into my eyes. "So, what if you probably hurt someone that you care about in order to advance more than a few levels, would do that?"

I scoffed. "It really just depend on who that person is. I done fucked over a lot of people I cared about because I didn't see them in my future. I feel like if you can't see that person in your future, or that person is of no benefit to your advancement, if you don't fuck them over, then they're just a casualty of war. A sacrifice that has to be made. Fuck 'em. It's all about surviving for the riches, nah'mean? It is what it is." I kissed her forehead and sat up. My dick was getting hard again and it felt sore. I knew her pussy had to feel the exact same way.

She sat up and the covers fell off of her chest, exposing her succulent breasts with the huge nipples that were as usual, erect. "Jayden, what if I told you that I'm about to bust a major move that's going to get me a few million, and I told you that I was going to need you to be by my side afterwards because the heat will be intense? Would you roll with me?"

I frowned as I pulled my boxers up and tried to stop lusting over her. She had my hormones going crazy. "You talkin' millions. You should already know I'm down for the cause. What you need me to do? Knock a nigga head off or somethin'?"

She got on her knees and walked across the bed on them until she was standing in my face. "Look, cuz, I'm about my paper, and I gotta do it big. Long as I know that you rolling with me after I do what I do, then I'm finna go ahead and handle my business. I got that gangsta shit in me just like you do. That's why we rock so well together. The last thing I need to know is that no matter what, you're always going to love me. Is that the truth?" She looked deep into my eyes, holding my face in her small hands.

"I will. Handle yo' business, lil' mama, with no mercy. And when you need for me to step in, all you gotta do is holler."

Chapter 11

I'd been down in Atlanta for a full month and was starting to get used to the living down there when, at first, I never thought I was going to be able to because I was so used to living in the fast lane of the east coast. But the longer I stayed down there, the more I was able to get my footing. Not to mention that I was making money hand-over-fist just by fucking with Percy. He was one of them type of niggas that didn't like to get his hands dirty. I considered him a coward, and I figured I'd keep capitalizing off of him until Myeesha gave me the order to bust his brains, though I couldn't really tell how close she was to getting to the point.

She and I spent less and less time together because Percy always had her handling some form of business. I didn't really know what they had going on behind the scenes and I really didn't care, just as long as he kept my pockets filled with cash and kept his hands off of Myeehsa.

One day, I was in the pool, floating on one of the blue inflatable lounge chairs, smoking on a Cuban cigar filled with weed that Percy had provided me, when Myeesha walked into the backyard with some papers in her hands. "It's done, Jayden. All of it is done. We got married two days ago at the court, and these papers have made it official." She said, taking off her Chanel sunglasses, and setting them on the glass table next to the iced pitcher of pink lemonade.

I blew a cloud of smoke into the air, looked over to her and smiled. "That's what's up."

She stopped at the head of the pool, pulled her Chanel dress over her head, dropping it to the ground, then pulled her long hair back into a pony tail, and got into the pool, swimming over to me while I floated on my back in the deep end, chilling like a boss. When she got to me and popped her head out of the water, she spat to the right of us. "Don't you understand what this means? Huh?"

I nodded. "Yeah, it mean that I'm finally finna be able to knock yo' nigga head off. It's about time." I laughed and sipped from my pink lemonade.

She shook her head. "Not only that. It means that I got access to all of his money. We ain't ever gotta worry about hustling the hard way. From here on out, it's gon' be smooth sailing. You got my word on that." She tried to hug me but wound up putting so much pressure on the side of the lounge chair that she flipped me into the water.

I threw the blunt first, and then the glass of lemonade. Then, I started thrash violently in the water. Having never learned how to swim, I was on the verge of panicking. "Uhh, uhhh, uhhh."

Myeesha grabbed my waist and tried to calm me down until I was able to grab on to the floating lounge chair and kick my legs so I could get the fuck out of that pool. I was heated as hell. I could hear her laughing over my shoulder and it only added to my irritation. I think I was more embarrassed than anything else though. But finally, I made it to the side of the pool where I climbed out with water dripping off of me. My shorts molded to my penis, and the sun started to bake my back right away. I grabbed my Gucci towel off of the table and wiped my face.

Myeesha got out of the pool in her one-piece bathing suit with her nipples rock hard. The crotch band cuffed her cat like it owed it some money. She walked over to the table with a big smile on her face; both dimples out on each cheek. She held her hand up when she got close to me. "I'm sorry, Jayden. I didn't mean to flip you in. Can you forgive me?" She asked, placing her hand on my chest.

I ain't wanna talk about that shit because it wasn't gon' do nothing but make me mad. "So, when am I killing this nigga? I wanna get this shit over with." I couldn't contain the anger in my voice. I was trying my best to calm down, but it just wasn't happening.

Before she could answer my question, Percy walked swiftly out of the house with his eyes wide open. "Jayden, I need to holler at you right now. This cannot wait." He looked like he was on the verge of losing his mind.

Myeesha walked over to him to try and console him. "What's the matter, baby? Is there anything that I can do to help?" She cooed.

He waved her off. "N'all, not right now. I just need to talk to him alone. Go in the house for a minute." He frowned looking, down at her.

She lowered her head and sighed. "Okay, well, I guess I'll talk to you later, Jayden. We need to finish that conversation because it's very important. Awright?"

I nodded, and once again tried to control my anger because I ain't like the way that fool Percy had just came at her. All she'd tried to do was console him, and he wound up shitting on her. That had me heated to the utmost.

She stopped and picked up her dress, looked over her shoulder at me, then made her way into the mansion with her shoulders hunched. Both ass cheeks jiggled with each step that she took.

I looked over at Percy and mugged him. "Yo, from now on, you don't come at my cousin like that, kid. She was trying to make sure you was straight. Nah'mean?" I felt my heart pounding in my chest.

He looked taken aback. "That's my bad, Jayden. I ain't mean nothin' by it, but it's so much shit that's going on. We gotta holler at Locust tonight, or the Crips gon' bomb by clubs, man." He wiped sweat from his forehead and started to pace in front of me.

I slid my Polo white beater over my head, and tucked it into my shorts. "Who the fuck is Locust, and what the Crips want it with us for? I thought they beefed with Bloods?" I was confused 'cause I really didn't do all that gang banging shit. I was a cut-throat type nigga, especially since me and Nico had fallen out. I mean, I still had a lil' love for Kilroy, but that was it.

Percy shook his head. "I guess that message got back to him about what you did to Dream and one of his hitters. He say he feeling like you trying to come down from Philly and take over the A, so y'all need to meet so y'all can get an understanding or he gon' bring heat to me just to prove a point. Man, I got too much invested on Peachtree Street. Then, on top of that, I'm looking to open the Queen of Diamonds in two weeks. I can't have them niggas busting up my operations." He took a deep breath and exhaled slowly. "Then, if that ain't enough, I got the law all over my ass from that shit with Dream. As long as he's missing, the deal can't go through. Supposedly, they got an anonymous tip that I had something to do with his disappearance. I'm freaking out right now, man. They're talking about freezing all of my bank accounts, and they didn't even fully explain why that is. What are we gon' do?"

I looked over at this nigga, wound back and slapped the shit out of him. *Bam!* "Shut the fuck up. You sounding like a real bitch right now, nigga!" He fell over the table and knocked the pink lemonade onto the concrete, shattering the pitcher and sending its contents all over my bare feet. That got me even more irritated. "Get yo' punk ass up."

He shot to his feet, holding his face, looking me over as if he really wanted to kill me, but I knew he didn't have the heart. He was just a bitch nigga with a whole lot of money. "You ain't have to put yo' hands on me, Jayden. That's some bullshit." He turned the shade of red, and I didn't give no fuck.

I looked over and saw that Myeesha was watching us from the doorway. "First of all, fuck that Locust nigga. I'm 'bout whatever he 'bout and I'll meet him anywhere at any time, by my-muthafuckin'-self. He is right, I am here to take over. Secondly, this ain't no *we* type shit, my nigga. You supposed to be the boss, which means you're supposed to always be two moves ahead of anyone's that you have me make on your behalf. Seeing as you don't know what the fuck you doing, fall back and let me take the lead. Call that bitch nigga and tell him that I'll meet him anywhere he wanna meet." I wiped my mout, and scoffed at Percy. I hated soft niggas. I couldn't wait to body his punk ass.

He continued to hold his face. "Aight, man, but I think y'all should meet somewhere in the open. I know how you get down, Jayden, but Locust get down the same way. He got an upper hand on you because his Crip niggas ride and die for him, whereas you're on your own down here and they can catch you slipping in any way. I'm not saying you can't hold your own, but you have to be smart, for both of our sakes."

I picked my phone up from the chair I'd been sitting in, then looked over to Percy and nodded. "Yeah, you might be right. Just set that shit up and I'll be there. Then we'll take it from there."

* * *

That night, I got a text from Shawn saying that she was in Atlanta and that she needed me to pick her up from the Greyhound bus station. She would be arriving at eleven that night. That completely caught me off guard because I had never let her know where I'd moved to. Secondly, for her to have already gotten on the bus said that she had a lot of faith that I would not shit on her. I sat on the edge of my bed in Percy's mansion for a long time before I responded.

I pulled the Bentley into the bus station's parking lot at 11:15 and saw her immediately. She stood right in front of the depot with a book bag on her shoulder. I pulled into a parking space. I jumped out of the whip and threw my arms in the air. "Yo, Shawn! Over here, ma!"

As soon as she saw me, her eyes lit up, and then she took off into a jog, running directly into my arms and laying her head on my chest. "Jayden, they killed my son. Them muthafuckas killed my son, and had I not made it out of the house, they would have killed me too." She whimpered with tears streaming down her pretty face.

I held her tighter and rubbed her back. "Who are you talking about?" I was confused and wondered why Kilroy had not reached out to me and told me this bit of information.

She sniffed snot back into her nose and swallowed. "Them Mexicans. They're the same ones that stabbed Naz up in the county jail about three days ago. I don't know what's going on, but I'm not safe in Philly. You gotta protect me." She cried.

I hugged her tighter and sighed. I looked around the parking lot trying to get a hold of myself before I ushered her into the Bentley and closed the passenger's door. Then, I jogged around to the other side, got in and pulled off. "What's good with Kilroy? He ain't been over to check on you or nothin'?" I asked, glancing from the road to her.

She shook her head. "Ever since you left, ain't nobody been by to check on me. It's like I don't even exist. Its messed up 'cause I don't know what's going on between those Mexicans and you guys, but they're taking it out on me and have killed Naz Junior. We were in the house sleeping, Jayden, and them bitches set it on fire. They tried to cook us alive. Now my baby is dead." She lowered her head and covered her face with her hands.

I noticed that before she did that, she had to squeeze her eyes together real tight in order for water to come out of them. I reached over and rubbed her back. "Yo, it's good now, ma. You're safe and we gon' figure this shit out."

She shook her head again. "You don't understand, Jayden. I don't have anybody to turn to. Naz got stabbed up a few days ago and they still have yet to give me an update on him. I don't know whether he's dead or alive. What am I going to do?" She broke into a fit of tears.

I was so caught off guard that my brain felt like it was on the verge of shutting down. I couldn't believe that Kilroy had not reached out to me in regards to this situation. "Yo, how did you know where I was?" I asked, looking over at her.

She froze for a second and then started to cry louder, covering her face with her hands. "I don't know what to do, Jayden. Please, just tell me that you got my back."

I shook my head and repeated the question. "Yo, Shawn, answer me. How did you know where I was?" Now I was mugging her with obvious anger. I could feel my temper rising.

"You told me before you left where you were going. Don't you remember?" She wiped her tears from her cheeks and became real fidgety.

I shook my head again. "N'all, ma, that's a damn lie. I ain't tell nobody where I was going, so tell me what's really good." I grabbed the .45 from my waist and placed the barrel against her cheek as I pulled into the alley right across from where the old Bank Head projects used to be before they were torn down in 2011. I drove halfway down the alley and threw my whip in park, cocking the hammer. "I ain't gon' ask you again."

She swallowed and blinked tears. "Okay, okay. Don't kill me, Jayden. Naz making me do this shit.

He's working out a deal with the Feds. He said that if I can come down here and feed you that story that I would be able to get under you and get you to confess some things that you've done. The Feds have been tracking you real close ever since you touched down in Atlanta. I don't know what they're up to, but they want you real bad. You and Kilroy. They know that you are somewhere in Atlanta, and they sent me here to set you up but I was against it from day one. Please believe me, Jayden. Naz is making me do this; I swear."

I ripped her shirt down the middle, then her bra, causing her titties to fallout. I was searching for a wire of some sort but didn't find any. I even made her lean forward so I could check her back and everything. At my conclusion, I slammed her back into my seat. "So, what do they want you to do, Shawn, and don't lie."

"No, I won't. I was supposed to come down here and contact them after I met up with you. I wasn't supposed to leave Philly until the morning, so as far as they know, I'm still up there. I really was caught between telling you what was going on and following the orders that Naz had given me. You know I've always been loyal to you, Jayden. I would've never done this if I didn't feel like Naz would kill me if I didn't."

I exhaled loudly and tried to think everything through thoroughly but my brain was fucking me over. If the Feds were tracking me like she said they were, how much did they really know, and how much time did I have until they closed in and indicted me for the list of things that I'd done? I was so confused and worried at the same time. They had to have known that Shawn had touched down. Our phones must've been tapped, which meant they were a few steps ahead of me.

"So, are you sure that once you touched down you were supposed to touch basis with them? Did they give you a number or something?"

"Yeah, it's in this phone that they gave me inside of my book bag." She reached into the backseat and grabbed the bag, unzipped it and pulled out an iPhone 10. She scrolled down the log until she stopped on a number that said, *Feds*. I thought that was almost too convenient. "Here you go." She handed the phone to me. "They gave it to me last week."

I took the phone and slid it into my pocket. My mind was all over the place. I looked back at her, and all I could see written across her face was betrayal. I had always had a lot of love for her, and I'd always been there for her as best as I could. I knew that Naz had to have been behind the whole plot. I just couldn't understand why she'd go along with it. I shook my head, then grabbed her around the neck with my right hand.

She started to smack at it. "Ack! Ack! Let me go! Ack! Please! Ack!"

I placed my left one around her neck then straddled her, squeezing with all of my might, digging my nails into her throat. Cardi B's "I Like It Like That" played out of my speakers. My vision went hazy as I reminisced on our past. She struggled against my grip with her eyes bugged out of her head. Her legs kicked under me. Tears dropped out of her eyes and ran down her cheeks, stopping at my wrists before dripping off of them. Tighter and tighter I squeezed until her struggles got weaker and weaker. Still, I didn't let up until she dropped her hands away and her body went slack. I sat back in the driver's seat with my chest heaving. I didn't know what I was going to do next. I had never felt more lost in my life.

I got out of the car and opened my backdoor, before coming back around and pulling her out, laying her on the floor in the back, then thought it'd be better to throw her in the trunk, which is what I did. After that, I slowly pulled out of the alley and drove back to the bus station, where I saw that there were nine buses lined up, nearly ready for departure. I walked over to the one that had a sign saying that it was headed for Los Angeles. I took the book bag that Shawn had carried with her, and handed it to the bus driver that was loading bags into the bottom of his bus. Without even looking up at me, he grabbed the bag and tossed it under there along with the others. As he turned to his left to pick up one of the suitcases that was to the left of his foot, I took the cellphone and tossed it into the bottom of the bag carrier and walked away with sweat pouring down my back, and my palms itching inside of the leather gloves. I didn't know how much time that would buy me, but I was going to have to make the best of it.

Ghost

Chapter 12

I stepped into the dimly-lit Italian restaurant, feeling the .45 poking into my hip as Percy walked in front of me, looking as if his knees were about to buckle at any second. I looked to my left and saw the Italian woman on stage humming along to the music that came out of the speakers. Behind her was a band that did their best to imitate one of Frank Sinatra's old classics. To my right sat a bunch of white people that looked to be enjoying their meals in the romantic setting. There were candles on top of their tables, and most of the couples I saw were holding hands or looking across the table at their mate in a loving fashion.

We made it about fifty feet inside of the restaurant when we were met by a Maître D' who held a tablet in his hand. "May I help you gentlemen?"

Percy nodded. "Yeah, we have a reservation for a party of four. It should be listed under Robinson."

The Maître D' scrolled down his log until he located the name, then he smiled. "Yes, I have you right here, sir. Please follow me right this way," he said in his Italian accent. He led us through the front of the restaurant until we made it to the back where there was a table with two men already sitting at it.

One of them was a dark-skinned man with long dread locks, and had Ray Ban glasses on his face. The man that sat next to him was also dark-skinned, but heavier. He had tattoos all over his face, so much so that it made him almost look dirty. I locked eyes with him right away and frowned.

Percy nodded at the Maître D' and slipped him a fifty. "Look, we back here talking business. Bring us your finest bottle of champagne, and make sure that we are not disturbed after that. Do you hear me?"

"He already know what it is, homeboy. You ain't gotta tell him shit. Look, Mane, fuck that champagne. Stay yo' ass out there and do like I told you when I first walked in this bitch. You know what's at stake here. Do I make myself clear?" The dirty-looking one asked, lowering his glasses so that the man could see his eyes. I noted that one of them were all white, as if he were blind in it.

The Maître D' bowed his head. "Very well, Mr. Locust. Don't you worry. I'll see to it that your wishes are carried out to the best of my abilities." He slowly backed away, and I could see him stopping and talking to the other Maître D' as he made his way back to his post in the front of the establishment.

I scoffed and looked down on the nigga that he had identified as Locust. "Now that was real rude. How you know we weren't thirsty?" I asked, looking from him to the other cat that was with him.

He picked up a bottle of Patron from the table and turned it up, looking at me over the top of it. "It don't matter if you was. This bitch is on my turf, and I don't let no muthafucka sip shit on my land until I get an understanding with 'em." He pointed at the two chairs across from him and his mans.

I grabbed one of the chairs from the table, pulled it back and sat down. Then, I snatched the bottle of Patron and took the top off, and turned that bitch up, taking long swallows, mugging Locust. His mans jumped up and put his hand under his shirt. Locust touched his arm and shook his head. I laughed to myself, finished my drink and burped loudly, just as Percy sat down next to me, looking like he was about to shit on himself.

"So, you must be the Philly nigga that everybody talking about. You come down to Atlanta for a specific purpose, homeboy?" Locust asked as his mans sat down and continued to glare at me from across the table.

I wiped my mouth with the back of my hand. "I come down to this bitch to get my piece of the pie, and ain't nobody gon' stop me from doing that. Nah'mean, kid?" I sucked my teeth and looked into the eyes of his mans. He looked real tough and all that shit, but I wondered how tough he'd be if I put that steel to his ass. That hammer always made tough niggas come on they periods like women, real quick.

Locust sat back and laughed, looking over at Percy. "This is a fucking joke, right? This is either a fucking joke, or this lil' nigga is out of his mind. Either way, we got heat for niggas like you down here in the A. The way you acting, you might not make it back to Philly."

"Especially if you give me the word, Capo. I'll bust his brains right now. Splatter his shit all over the table. You know I will."

Percy held up his hands. "Come on now, gentlemen, we're supposed to be here so we can get an understanding. There is no beef between either of us. We're businessmen and I'm sure that we can work things out so that everybody leaves here happy."

I was still mugging Locust's lil' hitta. In my mind this nigga had just threatened my life like it was sweet. I saw myself blowing his head off before he could do it to me. I was never the one to respond to threats real well. Locust was getting ready to say something when I cut him off. "Yo, let me guess something right now. Kid, you one of them hungry niggas in the hood that gotta do all that you can to please this nigga right here. You ain't yo' own man. You's a peon, and the only way you can do anything out here in the A is if this nigga right here give you the go ahead. You living off of his coattail, and without you wouldn't be shit but a bum ass nigga, am I right?"

He jumped up and pulled his shirt back so I could see the handle of his .9-millimeter. "Man, let me smoke this nigga, Locust. Fuck he think he is, Cuzz?" He lowered his eyes, looking down on me.

I grabbed the bottle of Patron and turned it up again, swallowing a nice portion of it, feeling the alcohol mix with the Oxy's and the Cuban Loud that Percy had hit me with. I was floating on air and didn't give a fuck about nothing at that moment. The Feds had my mind boggled, and the way I saw it I was living on borrowed time one way or the other. "You see, that's the difference between me and you. I don't gotta ask nobody to stank a nigga. If I want to, I'll just do it." I took the pistol out of my waist and set it on my lap under the table, feeling the beats of my heart speed up like they always did when I was on the verge of losing myself.

Locust looked up at his hitta and scrunched his face. "Nigga, sit yo' ass down. You're causing a scene. It's a time and a place for everything."

126

His hitta reluctantly took his seat, never taking his eyes away from me. I couldn't take niggas like him serious. Real killas didn't answer to nobody. They lived by the gun, and that was that.

Locust smiled, picked up the bottle of Patron and took a long swallow from it. "As crazy as this shit may sound, I like you, lil' nigga. I think you got plenty heart, and if it's true with what everybody saying about Dream and that nigga Kano, then it sounds like we can do business. Fuck them Blood niggas, Cuzz. I applaud you for giving them the blues." He laughed and drank from the bottle again.

Percy smiled. "Then we're good here. There is no problems between us?" He asked with a glimmer of hope.

Locust shook his head and pursed his lips. "Oh, hell n'all. Nigga, you still gotta come out yo' pockets. I said we can do business. I ain't say I was gon' let you slide on shit. You know it's rules in the A." He placed his elbows on the table and interlocked his fingers. "You was paying that fool Kano sixty gees a week. I'll take fifty, and it's only because Cuzz right there knocked off Dream and Kano. Or allegedly, I should say."

Percy exhaled loudly. "What I had going with Kano ain't got nothing to do with the Crips though. Far as I knew, we were supposed to had a treaty. My brother squashed shit with you niggas before he got locked."

Locust shrugged. "Fuck yo' brother. That nigga ain't here no more, and he can't save you. The fee is fifty gees. Pay up or I'm burning yo' shit down. Or, there is one thing that you can do and you ain't gotta worry about my niggas no more. In fact, if you do it, you'll have their protection for as long as you're in the A."

Percy opened his eyes wide. "Yeah, and what is that?"

Locust frowned. "The Onyx is in Cuzz territory. We been beefing with Dream's bitch ass for the last two years over that club. Now that he's out of the picture, you can just turn it over to us and go on about yo' business. No harms and no fouls. If not, we gon' burn that bitch down, Cuzz." Locust said, leaning all the way across the table in Percy's face.

I took my side of the table and pushed it forward with all of my might, causing it to slam into his chest, before I slapped my pistol on the table with the silencer already attached to it. Locust looked as if he was caught off guard, and his hitta scooted to the side and stood up, trying to decide on what to do because his Capo was trapped against the wall. I knew right then that dude wasn't no real killer. He was faking the funk. Had that been Kilroy, me, or even Nico, we would have emptied the clip in whoever had pulled that stunt. I missed Philly. I swear I did.

Locust tried to push the table away, then looked down and saw that the gun was pointed directly at him with a silencer on the end of it. His eyes got big, then he sat still, grunting under his breath. Percy took a big napkin and threw it on top of my piece. I was so high that I'd not stopped to even think about where we were. Luckily the restaurant was dimly-lit, and we were way in the back, close to the exit. There weren't any people in our section, and I think Locust had designed for it to be that way. Either way, I didn't give a fuck. I felt like I had a death wish. I couldn't get prison or the Feds off of my mind.

"Check this out, you bitch ass nigga. He ain't paying you shit 'cause he paying me for protection." I looked up at his mans. "Sit yo' ass down fo' I pop this fuck nigga across from me. Hurry up!" I growled.

He took his pistol out of his waistband and cocked it back. "Hell n'all, Mane. You done went too far, homeboy."

"Yo, tell son to sit his ass down before I count to three, Locust, or word is bond, on my mother, I'ma heat yo' ass up. Don't test me, kid. One, two."

"Mike-Mike, sit yo' ass down, man. Damn! Nigga, if he shoot me 'cause you on this bullshit, your family gon' pay the price, Cuzz."

Mike-Mike jerked his head back and frowned. "What? You talking like that, and this nigga got a gun on you. Man, fuck you, Cuzz." He put his pistol on his waist and waved Locust off, making his way out of the restaurant.

I started laughing. "That's the type of niggas you got riding for you, kid? Soft niggas that get emotional when you give them an order?" I scooted my chair back and sailed around the table until I was on the side of him. "Get yo' bitch ass up and let's go outside so we can talk like men. Come on." I ordered, trying to pull him up.

He jerked his arm away from me, jerked his shoulder and his glasses fell off of his face, exposing his white eye and the brown one that looked as if it was fading. "I ain't finna let you take me nowhere so you can kill me. I know how you get down, Cuzz. I ain't stupid. You gon' kill me, you gon' kill me right here, in front of all of these people!" He hollered at the top of his lungs. "Aye! This nigga got a gun and he trying to kill me!" He hollered.

"Jayden, let's get the fuck out of here," Percy said, grabbing my arm.

"You's a dead nigga, Percy. You is too, Jayden. Watch, Cuzz. Help! Help! He trying to kill me!" Locust screamed.

A bunch of the staff started to run back toward our area. I placed my pistol back on my waist, lowered my head and left out of the back exit with Percy in front of me. I couldn't believe the card that Locust had played. I felt like he'd out-thought me, and that made me angry. The back exit led to a bunch of tables and chairs that were in a Cabana-like setting. There were big umbrella-like tops on each of them, along with a gate that kept the area closed off from the Greek place that was directly next door, that I imagined was their competition.

I started to jog once we were out of the door. Then, I jumped over the gate right after Percy and wound up in the Greek restaurant's parking lot where Percy had parked his Benz truck. He ran to the driver's side door and opened it, then popped the lock for me to jump into the passenger's seat, started the truck and backed out in a hurry, slammed on the brakes, switched gears, and stormed out of the lot like a bat out of hell.

"Do you have any idea what you just did?" He hollered over at me with his eyes bucked.

I adjusted my seatbelt. "I stopped you from getting hoed, that's what it looks like to me. I don't know why you bow down to these niggas out here. They ain't on shit."

He made a left out of the parking lot and entered the busy street, after a pick-up truck allowed for him to. "Man, Jayden, that's not how shit works down here. I know you used to handling business a certain way back in Philly, but here in Atlanta, these niggas are grimy, they're cowards, and they don't let shit go. I know for a fact that fool Locust about to burn my club down. That nigga ain't about to take what you just did to him lying down. Every nigga in Atlanta gon' know about what happened to him. He ain't gon' have no other choice other than to clap back at us. Fuck! I should've known you was gon' handle this shit all wrong. I gotta figure this shit out." He shook his head and exhaled slowly, speeding onto the highway.

"Yo, on my word, kid, I ain't ever met a nigga as soft as you before. Word is bond, if you was in Philly, one of our grimy lil' niggas would've had you checking a bag too. I'm still curious to know how you made it this far without giving up all of your paper?" I scoffed at him and shook my head before glancing out of the window into the gloomy night. I wanted to get the fuck out of his presence. Just being around a nigga so soft was starting to make me feel irritated.

He drove on in silence for a long time before glancing over at me. "Say, Jayden, I ain't soft, man. I just like having money and living my life as drama-free as I possibly can. One thing that all rich niggas know is that you can't make the right amount of money consistently and beef at the same time. It's just impossible. When my brother was out, he did all of the beefing and I made the business moves. I didn't have to worry about nobody coming at me bogus because he was a pure goon like you. So, I ain't soft, I just ain't ever had a chance to learn to be a goon like y'all did."

I smiled and nodded. "Yeah, well, if you wasn't fucking with my cousin Myeesha, I'd make yo' ass pay me a hunnit bands a week 'cause you are soft, my nigga. That's my word." I glanced into the rear-view mirror and saw that we were being followed by two blue 1964 Chevy Impalas. I knew from experience that most Crip niggas, especially the ones in the south and out in Cali had a thing for old school whips. I didn't know why, but they just did.

"Damn, a hunnit gees? That would be fucked up. I'd have to have a nigga like you get rid of yo' ass if that was the case. Luckily I ain't gotta worry about all of that." He laughed. "Man, I'm in a bind though."

"Yo, kid, you still got that Tech under yo' seat right?" I asked, looking in my rear-view mirror.

He nodded. "Yeah. Fifty shots. Why? What's really good?"

I unclicked my seatbelt, crouched and reached between his feet to grab the handle of the Tech. "Get off on that exit over there. These fuck niggas been following us ever since we left that Italian joint."

Chapter 13

"Alright, let me out right here and drive off. Come back in literally two minutes. Don't be late, nigga, or I'ma bust ya' ass. Word is bond." I slammed the door as he peeled off. I ducked on the side of the burgundy Eddie Bauer truck that was parked on the street of the one-way.

The block was dark, and the reason I'd chosen it was because there were no streetlights on it. I knew that I would be able to do my thing without so much as being detected by the people that lived on that street. I cocked the Tech and waited for the blue Chevys to bend the corner in search of Percy's Benz, and just like clockwork, I saw the first turn onto the street with its top dropped, cruising slowly as if on a hunt. The driver turned the lights off and made their way down the block.

I scrunched my face, got on one knee in front of the Eddie Bauer's bumper and peeked down the street again, just in time to see the second car turn on the block, following closely behind the first one. Now I was nodding with a big smile on my face. I took a deep breath and blew it out slowly. With my back against the bumper I scooted along it, peeking one more time to see how close they were. I waited until I could feel the vibrations of the cars under me feet. The air got thick. I could smell the exhausts from their pipes. As soon as the first car slowly breezed past me I jumped up and aimed for the occupants inside of the droptop.

Bocka, bocka, bocka! Bocka, bocka, bocka! Fire spat from the barrel of my Tech as it jumped in my hand. I watched blood splatter against the windshield of the first car, before it crashed into a parked van up ahead. I turned to the car behind me and aired at they ass next. *Bocka, bocka, bocka, bocka. Bocka, bocka, bocka.* "Bitch ass niggas!" My bullets shattered their windshield. The second one hit the driver right in the middle of his forehead.

He fell forward with his face on the horn, blaring it for all to hear. I noted that more than three houses flipped their lights off. I imagined everybody inside of those houses dove to the floor like I'd been taught when I was a kid.

Boom, boom, boom, boom, boom! One of the occupants in the backseat of the second car returned fire before jumping out the whip and taking off running in the other direction. I wanted to air at him but couldn't get a good shot because he was running in a zig zag line. I ducked and backed away from the Eddie Bauer truck, staying low to the ground until I made it to the sidewalk with my eyes on both whips. One of the occupants of the first car jumped out of it with a sawed off shot gun in his hand. As soon as he saw me, he let that bitch ride. *Boo-wa. Boo-wa. Boo-wa.* I heard one of his bullets slam into one of the car doors, rocking the vehicle. I turned to run in the other direction, tripped and slammed my face right into the curb. My teeth crashing into the concrete. It hurt so bad that I felt like screaming. I got up and took off running.

Boo-wa. Boo-wa. He aired at me. I jumped over a chain linked fence and ran alongside a gangway, before winding up in somebody's back yard that had a kiddie pool inside of it. I kept on running, pulled my phone out of my pocket and texted Percy to let him know that I would be coming out on the other side of the avenue. I ran my tongue over my upper row of teeth and felt them fold inward. My heart felt like it was about to stop beating.

* * *

"You see this shit? Huh? All because I was fucking with this nigga!" I hollered, spitting blood into the sink and looking into the mirror at Myeesha and Miah. I was heated and ready to kill something.

Miah picked up the two teeth that I'd pulled out of my mouth and held them in her hand. She pulled on my shoulder so that I could face her. She then lifted my upper lip and shook her head.

Myeesha stepped on the side of her. "It don't even look that bad, do it, Miah?"

Miah nodded. "Hell yeah. This is fucked up. Jayden was a dime looking nigga, but now he look like a base head. We gotta get this shit fixed ASAP. Fuck that." She said, sucking my blood off of her thumb.

I jerked away from her and looked in the mirror, lifting my head so I could see into my mouth. I'd lost both of my two front teeth. I looked horrible. I was missing my gap-toothed grin already. Now it looked like I had a hallway in my mouth. "Man, I should go in there and beat yo' nigga ass, Myeesha! I ain't playing either. Had I never went with that weak ass nigga, I wouldn't be looking like this right now. Then it took forever for his punk ass to come back around and scoop me!" I hollered, feeling my temper start to boil over.

Percy had not come to pick me up until ten minutes after I texted him. By that time, the whole area was infested with police. I had to hide under a dirty ass Geo Metro until he decided to pull up and get me. I wanted to kill that fuck nigga.

Percy stepped into the big bathroom with a phone to his ear. "Calm down, Jayden, I got one of the best dentists in the state of Georgia on the phone, ready to fix your problem as soon as morning if you want. He said as long as you get to him by then, he will be able to push them back in, and they will lock. So, you should be good to go. What do you say?" He asked, looking at my reflection.

I turned around to face him. "Book the muthafucking appointment, and he better be telling the truth, Percy, or word is bond, I'ma bust ya' ass, nigga, like I promised." I turned back to the mirror and ran my tongue across my gums.

Myeesha came and grabbed my hand. "Let me talk to you for a second, Jayden, 'cause I see that you're on edge, and knowing you, ain't no telling what you're about to do." She said this as we were passing Percy who was still on the phone, booking my appointment.

I mugged him with hatred, all the way until we got to the end of the hallway and made our way past the maid that was vacuuming the big rugs that lined the hall.

We got to the bedroom that I was staying in. Myeesha closed the door and looked me up and down. "What the fuck is your problem, lil' cousin?"

"What?" I frowned, growing angrier by the second.

"You heard me. You're walking around here like you're losing your fucking mind. Do you want to blow everything up and forfeit everything that we've worked so hard for?" She asked, pacing in front of me.

I walked over to my dresser and pulled out a clean face towel and placed it up against my bleeding gums. "I'm sitting here bleeding over yo' nigga and you making it seem like I'm the one with the problem. Man, miss me with that bullshit. I'm serious." I'd never put my hands on any female other than Shawn, and I was wishing that I never had to do that, but the way I was feeling in that moment, I felt like I could have kicked Myeesha's ass for coming at me like that.

I was already having a hard time thinking clearly because I felt like I was digging myself a bigger hole every single day. A hole so big that I honestly didn't know what to do anymore. I knew I had to get the fuck out of Atlanta though, and I needed more drugs in my system. Every time I blinked, I saw either Shawn or Nico's face and it was starting to get the better of me. Then, whenever I dozed off, Poppa would help them to haunt me. I was losing myself, and I didn't have anywhere to turn. On top of all of that, every time I heard a loud, off-putting noise I imagined that it was the Feds coming to get me. It was the worst feelings in the world if you asked me.

Myeesha covered her face, then took her hands away. "Got-damn it, Jayden. I got this fool thinking that them people are going to be auditing him real soon, so he's going to empty out his accounts and put all of that cash up in here. Now, I need him to do that so I can give the order for you to finish his ass, then we can go on about our lives. We're too close for you to fall apart at the seams right now. Don't you understand?"

I slid the plate of crushed Percocet from under my bed and sat it on my lap, took my pinky nail and tooted it hard up first my right nostril, and then my left. I pulled on my nose as the numbness began to course through me. I needed the pain to stop. My gums were pounding along with the pain of my soul. "Yo, it's good. I'ma be alright. I just gotta get my head together then we can go through with the plan, nah'mean?" I separated the powder into two lines, looking over at her.

She lowered her eyes. "Oh my God. What is wrong with you, Jayden? Are you losing your mind or something? I've never seen you like this before?"

I tooted up both lines hard, and coughed which made spit cloud my mouth before swallowing it, feeling the numbness all in my throat. "I'm going through a lot of shit right now, Myeesha, but don't worry. You know I'll bounce back." I put the plate on the floor and grabbed a blunt off of my dresser, sparking it right away.

Now the vision of my mother was eating at me. I saw her slit throat, the roaches that crawled all around her body, and then the scene at the lakefront played before my eyes when she'd stood firm and protected a pregnant Whitney from a group of young hoes that thought it was sweet until she got in their asses. Damn, I missed her. My eyes got watery. I inhaled and sat against the dresser with hazy vision.

Myeesha came over and stood in front of me, and placed her hand on the side of my face. "Jayden, I love you, lil' cousin. I can only imagine what you're going through because you have been through a lot. But you need to know that you aren't alone. You don't have to feel alone, and if you need to open up to Somebody, I'm right here with arms wide open. I swear. Do you believe me?"

I looked down at her and took a puff of my blunt. "Myeesha, I understand the game. We all got our different forms of controllers that we operate with. Right now, you're just trying to make sure that yours isn't defective, and I'm telling you that I'm good. I got that nigga. I just fell off for a minute. You handle what you have to. Make that fool empty his accounts, then we'll go from there. I'm good, I promise." I ran my tongue across my gums once again and wanted to flip out, even though I couldn't really feel my gums. The fact that there were no teeth there was heart-wrenching.

Myeesha looked into my eyes, stepped on her tippy toes, and kissed my cheek. "Well, I don't know what's going on in that big brain of yours, but you had better know how much I love you, Jayden. Don't get it twisted. It's still all about mine and youradvancement. Fuck everything and everybody else." There was a loud banging on the door. She turned on her heels and walked over to it. "Who is it?"

"It's Miah. I need to talk to Jayden for a minute. Are you guys about done in there?" She hollered.

"We'll be out in a minute. Go somewhere and sit down until then, Miah, damn." She rolled her eyes and walked back over to me, wrapping her arms around my neck. "I know you fucked her too, Jayden, and I knew you would, so I ain't even tripping about that. It is what it is." She kissed my cheek again.

I grabbed her small waist and held it, smiling. "Yo, if it ain't no big thang, then why you bring it up?"

She shrugged. "No reason. I just wanted to let you know that I knew, and I don't care. I'd rather for her to be doing that shit with you, than them two lil' girls she always frolicking with. To be honest, I thought my lil' sister was gon' wind up being a lesbian like most of these hoes in Atlanta. But I see the way she watches you when you're in the room. You got her nose wide open. I've never seen her look at any male like that, which lets me know that you put that grown dick on her lil' ass." She laughed. "You just love that forbidden shit, don't you?" She kissed my lips and stepped closer into my embrace, looking up at me.

I cuffed her ass and massaged the cheeks like I had a habit of doing to her and her sister. It felt like the kind of asses that they had should be rubbed on at all times. You had to appreciate them. Nothing else made sense to me. I kissed her neck and took a step back. "Yo, you already know how I am 'cause you're the same way. If you had a pipe, you'd a been fucked that lil' fresh pussy too. Now, lie and say you wouldn't have." I dared.

She shook her head and laughed. "Yeah, whatever. Just get your head right so we can finish what we started. It's almost over."

She made her way to the door and was about to open it when I stopped her. "Say, Myeesha. This something I was wondering. What ever made that fool Percy marry you at the courthouse instead of in a church like you'd previously planned?"

She smiled and licked her lips. "Well, let's just say that it would have taken too long. I need to be rid of this nigga, cousin. I'm trying to be laid up on a beach somewhere with you, doing the most, and hopefully Miah will be there trying to get in where she fit in too." She laughed again before opening the door and closing it behind her.

As soon as she left, I walked over and locked it, went into my closet and pulled out my safe. After punching in the digital combination, I opened it to reveal the $1.1-million in cash there. I closed my eyes and opened them. Sniffed at the air inside of the safe before closing it back. I had to get the fuck out of Atlanta as soon as we finished Percy. I had to find a new spot where I could lay low and duck the Feds until I could figure some things out. I closed my safe, pushed it back into the closet and sat on the edge of my bed, rocking to get my mind to calm down. There had to be a way out of the jam that I was in. There were the Bloods, the Crips, and there were the Feds. Three of the most powerful crews in America, and I was beefing with all three. I had to figure out a way to conquer at least the deadliest one. My life and my survival depended on it.

Ghost

Chapter 14

The next day, at five in the afternoon, I came from under the drug induced spell that the dentist had me under, to sit up in the chair and look at my new grill in the mirror. My head felt a little foggy, and my teeth were still numb along with my tongue, but I felt good enough to see what was good with my new smile.

Myeesha smiled and kissed me on the cheek. "Now that's how niggas do it down in the A. Twenty-foe Carat gold all around. You look like a boss, Jayden, just like you are." She said, kissing my cheek again.

I cheesed. I had the dentist take out my whole grill and replace them with 24-carat gold teeth. My shit was shining harder than the sun on a cloudless day. I nodded. "Even though I know I might not ever be allowed back in Philly because of this bullshit, it looks good."

Percy stepped forward and shook the short white man's hand and nodded at him. "Well, for thirty-two thousand dollars it better. They charged me a thousand a tooth. It's supposed to shine as hard as it is. Yo' Philly niggas will understand, and if they don't, show 'em the reciept." He joked.

I looked up to his ass and curled my lip. "Yeah, nigga, you just let me worry about my Philly kids." I made my way out of the chair with Miah helping me.

"You do look good though, Jayden. I didn't think you would, but I gotta admit, you're fly." She smiled and bit into her botom lip. "Can we rollout so I can holler at you now?"

I put my arm around her neck and looked over my shoulder at Myeesha, who rolled her eyes. "Yo, we will holler at y'all a lil' later. I'ma see what's good with her for a few hours."

Myeesha grabbed her purse off of the couch across from where I had been laid up, and rushed to my side, placing her lips against my ear. "Please don't get into no more trouble, Jayden. I'ma have him take care of that business as soon as possible. You got my word on that." She hugged my right side and walked back over to Percy and kissed his lips. "Thank you for taking care of him for me, daddy. I owe you one."

I remembered feeling sick on the stomach as I left the dentis'st office, with the teeth that they'd taken out of my mouth in a small Ziploc bag. There was no way I was about leave any pieces of me behind. I was superstitious that way.

We stepped out of the office and into the hot summer day. The sun was shining bright, and there was a cool little breeze that allowed for it to be just the right temperature. I led Miah to the car and opened the door for her. Then, I waited until she got in and closed the door before climbing in on my driver's side.

She leaned over, grabbed the back of my head, and sucked all over my lips, running her tongue into my mouth. If I could have felt it,   I was sure it would have been really good, but my entire face was numb. I saw her tongue shoot out more than once though, and I could hear her moaning into my ear. "Jayden, I want some of you. I been feening for your body ever since you climbed from between my legs.

Let's go and get a Telly so we can do the most." She whispered, then licked my earlobe again.

I started the car and pulled it out of the parking spot. "Yo, that sounds good, lil' mama. I been wanting to hit that shit again anyway. But in addition to that, I can tell that there is something really on your mind. You wanna talk about it?" I placed my right hand on her thick thigh and squeezed it.

She was wearing this short, Eves St. Laurent dress that barely covered her thick thighs. They were exposed and I could tell that she'd rubbed some kind of expensive lotion into her skin because she was popping, and smelled even better. I didn't give a fuck if I was dying from multiple gunshot wounds, if she wanted to fuck even at that time I would have been all for it.

She sucked on her bottom lip and placed her hand into my lap to squeeze my pipe tight in her hands. "Instead of talking, wouldn't you rather be ten inches deep in this fresh pussy?" She squeezed my dick again, then leaned over to kiss my lap before sitting back and pulling her dress all the way up, exposing the fact that she didn't have no panties on, and that she'd recently shaved her pussy bald. She slid her hand between her legs and stroked her lips, opened them and put two fingers deep into herself, moaning with her eyes closed.

I brought her fingers up to my mouth and sucked them clean, trying my best to taste her salt, and praying that the novacaine would wear off soon. I had visions of eating that pussy for an hour straight without letting up. I loved the way that her and

Myeesha tasted. Maybe it was just the forbidden aspect of it all, but either way it worked for me.

"Yo, I'ma give you what you want, and then you gon' sit down and tell me what's really on your heart. You hear me, baby cuz?" I reached over to rub in between her gap while she opened her legs wider for me to do so.

* * *

She sucked all over my neck as I moved backward into the room after sliding the keycard in and out of the door. I started to unbutton her blouse while she unbuckled my Gucci belt, and forced my shorts to my ankles so I could kick them off. She wiggled out of her blouse and unhooked her bra from the front. Her perky, golden titties spilled out into the open. Both nipples were erect, begging to be sucked on by me as she kissed my lips.

"I want you so bad, cuz. You should have never introduced me to that dick. Now I can't stop thinking about it every second of the day. It has become second to my money." She moaned.

I picked her up, forcing her to wrap her thick thighs around me like I loved for her to do. I held her up by those fluffy ass cheeks, feeling her hot pussy heat my torso. I took about ten steps and threw her back on the bed, peeled my beater off and dropped my boxers.

She laid on her back on the bed with her legs wide open and her dress around her waist. Her pussy fully exposed. She opened her lips for me to see. "Look at this little hole, Jayden. I know you wanna bust this in again. It's still fresh. You know that, don't you?"

146

In response, I dove on the bed and stuck my head between them thighs, opened her sex lips wide with my thumbs, and licked up and down her split; sniffing her up at the same time.

"Unnnh! Fuck, yes! Dis what I been missing. Cuz, do me right." She rubbed the top of my head and curled her pedicured toes.

I licked up and down her ass crack, then concentrated on her wet slit, sucking on her clit, while she squeezed her B cup titties together and twisted her nipples. "I love this shit, Miah. I love the way you taste, baby girl. Word is bond." I sucked both of her lips into my mouth, pulled on them, then opened her back up and stuck my tongue as far into her as it would go, darting my head back in forth.

"Unhh!" She opened her thick thighs wider, threw her head back and forced my face deeper into her. Raising her ass off of the bed, she was grinding into my face. "Unnnh! Shit, Jayden. It feel so good, baby! I need this all the time. All the fucking time!" She screamed, bucking into my face.

I sucked harder on her clit, nipping at it with my teeth, then I'd stuck it back into my mouth, pulling her lips all the way back to expose it more. Her cream dripped out of her and coated my chin. It went down my throat and I swallowed it hungerly, yearning for more.

"Yes, yes, eat me, cuz, eat me! Oooh-shit, eat this pussy. It's so wrong! It's so wrong! Uhh-shit, I'm cuming!" She hollered, bucking her hips from the bed and riding my face after trapping it with her thighs. "Uhhh-fuck!" She hollered, jerked into me, then tried to push me away.

I got on to my knees, turned her over onto her stomach and forced her back to the bed, pushed her left knee to her rib cage, then lowered my face right onto her ass cheeks, kissing all over them. She reached behind herself and spread them for me. I licked up and down her backdoor, sucking on the asshole, sticking my tongue into the little crinkle, opening it up so I could get further into her body.

"Ohhh shit, Jayden. Holy fuck! Oh my God! You're so gross! Ooh-a! Baby, you're so gross. I can't take it. I can't take this shit." She reached under herself and started to play with her clit.

I slid two fingers into her ass from the back, fucking them in and out of her before licking into it again. Then I trailed my face down and moved her fingers out of the way with my chin so I could suck on her jewel again, sucking it into my mouth loudly like a sliver.

"Uhhh-fuck me now, Jayden. I can't take it. Fuck yo' lil' cuzzy right now. Fuck me hard, too, please!" She begged looking over her shoulder at me with tears in her eyes.

The only times I had ever seen her in an emotional state was when I was doing my thing to her lil' body. I found that amusing to say the least.

I fingered her hard and fast until she came against my eyesbrows. Her ass crashed into them while she humped backward into my mouth. As soon as she finished quivering, I got to my knees and pulled her up by her hips. She reached up under us, stroking my dick, moaning with her eyes closed before putting the head on her hot opening. I rubbed it up and down, watching the way it made her sex lips part before I pushed into them and sank my pole deep into her snatch, hitting the bottom of her womb right away. The scent of her ass and pussy wafted into the air. I could feel her juices drying up on my lips, and the way her ass jiggled every time I crashed into her drove me literally insane for the pussy. I got to wearing that ass out like a mad man— long-stroking her, taking in every inch of that kitty that was fresh and hot. That forbidden pussy was the shit.

She humped backward into my lap, impaling herself on my dick with her eyes wide open, looking back at me. "Un! Un! Un! Un! Fuck me! Fuck me! Harder, Jayden! Harder! Wreck this pussy! Wreck it! It's okay! Uhh-shit! It's okay!" She hollered out of breath.

I gripped that fat ass and slammed her back into me with all of my might. The impact caused her thighs to jiggle and shake. *Bam. Bam. Bam. Bam. Bam. Bam. Bam. Slap!* I hit her on the ass cheek with an open palm, riding her like a jockey. The pussy was gushing its juices. They poured out of her and dripped off of my swinging balls while I attacked her like I'd paid my last $100 for the pussy.

"I'm cuming, Jayden. I'm cuming, baby! Uhh-fuck, you be treating me like a hoe. Oooo-shit!" She screamed, threw her head back and slammed into me again and again. Every time she'd connect, her ass cheeks would open, and she'd flash me the crinkle of her asshole. It was light brown with small traces of hair all around it. For some reason that sight caused me to go harder.

I pulled her long hair, forcing her to arch her back and sped up the pace, digging deep into her belly from the back.

"Ahhhhh-shit! I'm cuming! I'm cuming! Oooh-you're killing me!" She screamed. She started to shake and fell to her stomach with me still going ham inside of her.

My dick pistoned in and out at full speed. She reached behind herself, opened her ass, and I couldn't take it no more. I gave her ten quick pumps, and then I was coming deep within that box, skeeting and skeeting. She rose her ass up to meet my thrusts, milking me for every drop of seed I had. I stayed on top of her for a full two minutes before I pulled out and slid onto my side, exhausted. Sweat poured down my back and I could see that her face was drenched in it as well, and we were in a well air-conditioned hotel room, so that wasn't the problem. I think because her pussy was so good and so tight that it just made me want to go hard. I mean, Myeesha had a shot too, but Miah's was killing hers to say the least, and I don't know why that was. Maybe it was because I knew I had been the only nigga to ever hit that shit.

She rolled over and laid on the top of me with her hot pussy on my waist, sucking on my earlobe. "I never thought I'd even like dick until you put this big muhfucka on me. Now it's all I want. You should know that Kenya and Kellis are mad at you 'cause we ain't played around ever since you broke my hymen. I'm serious too." She kissed my chest as she trailed her hand down and gripped my pipe that was slowly losing its strength.

"Shorty 'nem will be alright. It is what it is. Anyway, now that we fucked and did what you wanted to do, why don't you tell me what's really on your mind?" I said, kissing her on the sweaty forehead.

She leaned all the way down, sucked my dick into her mouth, and licked all around the head before popping it back out. "Aiight, but let me start from the top." She exhaled loudly, got up and placed her back against the headboard. "Before you came down here, that nigga Percy tried to rape me twice, and I had to fight his ass off both times by myself, even though Myeesha was standing right there the whole time." She shook her head.

I sat up and got out of the bed, putting my boxers on. "Yo, word is bond, I'm finna blow that nigga head off. Fuck that."

Miah got out of bed and rushed over to my side of the room with her titties bouncing around on her chest. "Wait, baby, let me finish, and then you can do whatever you want to this nigga. I gotta get this all out or I'm going to have a serious melt down. I'm not kidding." She said, blinking tears.

I wrapped my arms around her shoulders and pulled her into my embrace, holding her close. I'd never seen her cry before, and it was breaking my cold heart. "Yo, aiight, ma'. Go ahead and say what's good, but in the end, I'm just letting you know what it is. Ain't no nigga gon' fuck you over like that. I don't give a fuck who it is." I sat on the bed and pulled her onto my lap.

She bounced up and stood before me, looking into my eyes with her green ones. "Please, don't touch me right now. I just need to get all of this out."

"Aiight, gon' head." I sat back and flared my nostrils, feeling some type of way because she'd pulled away from me, when I lowkey needed to feel her warmth in that moment, but I had to allow her to be comfortable. It made sense, even if it hurt a little.

"Like I was saying. Before you came down here, he'd tried to rape me two times, and both times Myeesha was right there and she didn't help me get him off of me. In fact, I think she would have let him if he'd been successful." She squeezed her eyes together. "She'll let that son of a bitch do anything just be cause he has a lot of money. I've watched him do some awful things to her, and she let him." She shook her head and covered her face with her hands, crying into them. "Do you know that she made me go down on him way too many times for me to count, even when I told her that I didn't want to? That he disgusted me to the utmost?" She wiped her tears away and frowned.

I didn't even know what to say because I was so heated. I mean, I was seeing red. On one hand I wanted to leave and go hit that nigga up with about fifty slugs, then bend Myeesha over my knee and beat her lil' yellow ass until it was redder than a Blood nigga's flag. I couldn't believe that she'd allow for something like that to happen to her little sister. I was at a lost for words.

Miah took a deep breath. "I wanna make him pay, Jayden. I wanna make him pay for everything that he's done to me, and even my sister. I have to get him back, and the way that I want to do it will be epic. I swear that on my life." She turned to me. "I know I've asked you this before, but I'm going to ask again anyway. Is there anything that I could do that would make you stop loving me?" She looked into my eyes with a tear running down the right side of her face.

I wiped it away and shook my head. "Nothing, baby girl. You do whatever you gotta do, or whatever your heart tells you to do and fuck what anybody thinks about it. You gotta make the world kiss your ass and survive by any means. You really ain't got much of a choice other than to be a goon, especially if the muhfuckas that's supposed to be protecting you is allowing for a nigga to hurt you just because they got money. That's fuck shit! Deep within you is a cold-hearted monster. Channel her and don't worry about the consequences. You feel me?"

She nodded. "More than you know."

Ghost

Chapter 15

It took almost two months for Myeesha to bring her full plan into fruition. During those two months, I stayed as close as I possibly could to Percy, watching his every move. It seemed that every single day he got more and more paranoid and worried about what either the IRS or Locust's boys were going to do to him. I also noticed that he developed a heavy habit for cocaine. Anytime that we were alone, he'd have his nose in a pile of it, trying his best to snort away his problems. After all of the things that Miah had told me that he'd forced her to do, it took everything in me not kill him on more than a few occasions. I'd caught him time and time again watching her walk around the house. He'd follow her with his eyes, shaking his head while holding his crotch. The closer I paid attention to him, the harder it became to restrain myself. I'd never wanted to body a nigga as bad as I wanted to do him.

Myeesha's plan finally went into play early one Tuesday morning. I had been in the room recounting my bread, using the Money Machine that Percy had given me, and for the fourth time, my grand total had come to $1.7-million and some odd change. I was thinking that it was time for me to figure out what I was going to do with my life. Over the last few months, Miah had been talking more and more about leaving Atlanta altogether and shooting down to Miami where Kellis and Kenya's uncle had promised to sell her one of his clubs on the strip for $1-million even.

She'd gotten her friends to come up with $500,00 of it, and wanted me to chip in the rest, which I was very close to doing, especially after she showed me the seven bad ass females that were willing to go into her stable. They had all been her friends from back in high school. And as far as I could see, they all pledged their loyalties to her. Unbeknowst to me, Miah had been going to a technical college down in Atlanta where she was learning about business, and how to run her club succesfully. About a week after she came to me with the proposal to meet her halfway on the club deal, she started to try and teach me some of things that she had been learning all along, and I had to say that I was impressed.

Kellis was also a business major at Clark University, and she was a beast when it came to numbers and business development. They'd sat me down on more than occasion to lace me, and I did all that I could to follow what they were talking about, but I found it kind of hard. I mean, I'd never been one of them book smart type of niggas. I was strictly street. It's not to say that I was an idiot or anything. I just didn't have the patience for all of that shit. I loved fast money, and the faster the better. I was looking into getting into the stripping game only because she wanted to. If it was up to me, I would have stayed in the slums, getting how I lived until I met my Maker.

But this Tuesday, Myeesha knocked on my door twice and then let herself in. My entire bed was full of hundreds and fifties. It looked like I'd just robbed a bank and brought the spoils to Percy's mansion.

My first instincts were to grab the pistol off of my hip and aim it at the door, which is just what I did, until I saw that it was her and sighed in relief. "Fuck! You can't be doing that type of shit, Myeesha, damn." I said, shaking my head and taking the bundle of cash from the Money Machine's dispenser, placing it back into my safe that was opened at the foot of the bed.

"It's done, Jayden. He got all of his money in our safes downstairs. I mean, he left about two million in the banks so as not to bring too much attention, but there is at least five down stairs, and I got the combinations. I need his ass whacked, like ASAP, before he moves the money down to Decatur like he plans on doing this Friday. If you can get rid of him by tomorrow, or the day after, we'll be good. Trust me on this." She said, biting on her finger nail.

I took another bundle of cash and placed it neatly in my safe before looking over my shoulder at her from one knee. "So, I hit this nigga, then what? You don't think nobody gon' come looking for his ass? Huh?"

She shrugged. "I don't care if they do. The whole city of Atlanta knows that Locust and his crew of savges are looking to kill Percy. Who's to say that when he goes missing that they aren't the ones responsible?" She asked looking down on me with her piercing green eyes.

I picked up another bundle of cash, flicked through it, then placed it into my safe. I still had 90% of the bed to reload. "Yo, I really don't care. The whole reason I came down here is so I could handle this nigga for you, so that's what I'ma do. All you gotta say is what day you want it done and it's a done deal."

As soon as I finished those words, I heard the front door slam, and then it sounded like somebody was stomping their way up the steps. As soon as they got to the top, the same stomps could be heard coming down the hall. "Jayden! Jayden! Where you at, my nigga? I need to holler at you!" Percy yelled before stopping at my door and knocking on it.

Myeesha's eyes lowered. "Why not handle his ass tonight and get it over with?" She whispered leaning closer to my face.

I nodded. "I got you. Let me holler at this nigga, and just know that it'll be done. Handle yo' business, then we'll talk."

She nodded as the pounding began again on the door. She ran over and kissed my cheeks, then jogged over and placed her hand on the knob. "Open it?"

"Yeah, let me see what he talking about. I got you though. That's my word."

She opened the door and Percy walked into the room talking a mile a minute. "Bro, them punks done shot up my truck while I was on the eastside, hollering at one of my potnas. They say they gon' burn my club down tonight if we don't meet up with them by eight o'clock and sign over all rights to Locust. He said he willing to drop all grudges held against me, for the shit that you did to him and a few of his niggas, if I sign the property over to him and drop a hunnit thousand dollars. Man, I'm thinking about doing it to get this shit over with. I can't keep looking over my shoulder all day long."

Myeesha squeezed past him and made her way into the hallway, closing the door behind her.

I looked up at him from the side of my face. "Yo, where he trying to meet at kid?"

"The Onyx, on their turf. I don't wanna meet there because they can be on some bullshit. It's too dangerous. I just wanna give this nigga this scratch and get on with my life. I still got the Dollhouse and the Cheetah Lounge, and in a few weeks we'll open the Queen of Diamonds, so fuck that Onyx. It's too much drama that goes along with it." He looked at the bed and frowned. "Where you get all this shit from?"

I mugged him. "Nigga, don't worry about what the fuck I got or where it came from. You got more pressing issues to deal with. Do you got this nigga number?"

He nodded. "Of course. Why would you ask me that?"

"Because I want you to call him so I can speak with him. That's why." I stood up with about $10,000 in my hand and walked over to Percy. "Call him up right now. Hurry up so we can nip this shit in the bud."

Percy shook his head. "Man, fuck that, Jayden. I'm just gon' pay him and keep it moving. I know you. You gon' fuck around and get us killed."

I grabbed this nigga by his Versace shirt and balled it into my fist. "Bitch nigga, do like I say. I ain't asking you right now. Call him and hurry the fuck up. I ain't gon' tell you again," I said feeling my heart pounding in my chest. I tossed the ten bands on the bed and looked him up and down angrily.

"Aiight, aiight, damn. You need to calm down sometimes, kinfolk. It ain't that serious." He pulled out his iPhone 10, scrolled down the log until he found Locust's contact number, then he called him.

I snatched the phone from him and put it to my ear

Locust picked up with music playing in the background. "What up? Fuck nigga, you better be calling me because you ready to sign them papers, or else it's gon' get real for you and your homeboy. Believe that, shawty." I could hear him sucking his teeth.

"Ain't this the same bitch nigga that cried for help a few months ago? Now you all tough and shit, huh?" I laughed and frowned at the same time.

"Aw, so let me guess. Percy bitch ass ran to you about his lil' situation, huh? He think you gon' solve it for him? Well, I'm letting you know right now, nigga, ain't none of that shit going on. It ain't sweet. The only reason why both of you fuck boys still alive is because I want this club the legit way, and I'll make more money off of Percy breathing than I would with him dead. Plus, it's so many price tags on yo' head that you won't be alive for long. I know that for for a fact." He sucked his teeth again.

I scoffed. "Nigga, you done?" I asked, looking over to Percy as he paced nervously.

"I ain't gon' be done until I get what the fuck I want, so what's y'all reason for calling me?"

"Nigga, shut up. This what it is. Look, that's my club now, and if you want me to sign it over to you, then meet me there tonight at ten o'clock. I'll be sitting in my office waiting on you. Come holler at me like a man. That's all you gotta do."

He sucked his teeth again loud enough for me to hear. "Nigga, I done already told Percy that if he ain't signed them papers over to me by nine o'clock tonight, and dropped that hunnit bands, I'm burning that bitch down, and I don't give a fuck who in it. Play with me if you want to."

I laughed. "I ain't gon' keep doing this shit with you. Like I said, I'll se sitting in the office by myself at ten o'clock tonight. If you want these papers signed, then come and holler at me like a man. It's as simple as that. Other than that, nigga, kiss my ass." I hung up the phone and tossed it at Percy. "Here, nigga."

"That shit was so stupid, Jayden. What the fuck is your game plan, huh?" He frowned and walked toward me. He must've thought about it because stopped and remained still.

I laughed and walked toward him, watching as he took a step backward. "You know what? You's a bitch ass nigga, Percy, and I ain't feeling you, my nigga." I kneeled and grabbed my .45 from under the bed, stood up and pointed it at him.

He froze and threw his hands up at about shoulder-length. "Damn, Jadyen, what's all this about?" His eyes were bucked, and already I could see his knees shaking.

I walked up to him, swung my pistol with all of my might and knocked him out cold, splattering blood all over the money that was on the bed. He fell backward into the nightstand, just as Miah came through the bedroom door and saw what was going on. She put her hands up to her face in complete shock.

* * *

"Hand me them pliers, lil' cuz. I'ma show you how us Philly niggas get down when a muhfucka cross us or hurt somebody we love."

Percy struggled against his binds and shook his head. "Jayden, come on, man. I ain't did shit to you. I been hitting yo' hand ever since you been here. I make sure your cousins are straight, and I do the best that I can with everything. Please, I'm begging you from one man to the other, don't do this to me." He whimpered with sweat pouring down the side of his face.

I had his feet and hands bound to the chair with duct tape, and we were in his trusted dungeon. I know he had to feel like shit, but I didn't give no fuck. This nigga had hurt my lil' cousin, so he had to pay for his sins the hard way. I wanted her to be a witness to it all.

Miah handed me the pliers then walked over and stood in front of Percy, looking down at him with her face balled up. It had been the first time I'd ever seen her look somewhat unattractive, but I understood considering the circumstances. She grabbed his chin and held it in her small hand. "You put me through hell, Percy. From the moment I moved into this mansion with you and my sister, you didn't waste anytime going in on me, and I hate your guts for everything that you did!" She screamed, raising her hand and smacking him across the face.

His head jerked to the side with his eyes closed. "Fuck! Miah, please forgive me. I'm sorry, baby girl. I was—"

Smack! "Don't you ever call me that, you sick bastard. I'm not your baby girl. I'm nothing to you, and you're nothing to me. I hope my cousin kill your sick ass in cold blood, and I'm going to be right here watching." She took a step back.

"Please. I'm so sorry. I swear I'll do anything to make—"

I wrapped my arm around his neck, placing him in a headlock. "Open yo' mouth nigga, or I'ma put one in yo' brain."

"Please, don't do this, Jayden. I'm sorry, man. What the fuck y'all want me to do?" He hollered.

"Suffer the way I did. Take that shit like a man, Percy. Get his ass, Jayden." Miah said, looking on excitedly.

I held him by the neck and slammed the pliers it into his mouth, busting his lips. "Open up!"

"Aww! Awww!" He hollered, finally opening his mouth with blood running out of it.

I clamped the pliers onto one of his teeth before pulling it with all of my might, wiggling it this way and that. "Yeah, buddy, here this bitch come."

"Awww! Awww! Stop! Please! Awwww-fuck!" He jumped around in his chair, unable to break his binds as I pulled out the first two teeth and dropped them on the floor.

Afterward, I latched on to another and another while he hollered and screamed at the top of his lungs like a bitch. His entire chest was full of his blood. It oozed down his neck in thick globs, and I paid it no mind. I kept right on working, pulling the teeth out of his gums by the root.

Miah covered her eyes and peeked through her fingers every now and then at the gruesome scene. I could tell that it was a little much for her to handle, but she was doing everything that she could to push through, and finally I'd succeeded in taking out every last one of his teeth. They were all over the floor below him.

"Awww! This is fucked up, Jayden. This is fucked up. Why are you doing this to me?" He cried with a mouth full of blood.

I leaned down and picked up each tooth, placing it in a Ziploc bag. "You hurt my baby, man. You had to pay. I don't give a fuck how much money you gave me, nigga. That shit don't hold no weight with me." I cocked back and punched him, connecting with his chin, knocking him out cold once again.

Chapter 16

I duct taped Percy's wrists to the chair in his office at the Onynx. Then, I picked up the gas can and poured it all over his body and office. I mean, I emptied every bit of three gallons of the stuff, to the point that the carpet in his office made loud squishing sounds with every step that I took. Myeesha had already told me that Percy had never been in trouble with the law, so I was sure that they didn't have his DNA on file, or in their database. I had to bust a major move at his expense. It would be the only way I would be able to shake the Feds, and get on with my life in a new region. I still wasn't entirely sure what that looked like. All I knew was framing Percy was step one. Everything else should fall in line after that.

I walked over to him and opened the Ziploc bag full of my teeth, then placed ten of them on his tongue, finally placing the duct tape over his mouth.

As soon as the tape was in place, his eyes shot open, and he began to struggle against his binds. "Mmm. Mmm. Mmm. Mmm."

I smiled and used his phone to call Locust. It was 9:30; already past the deadline that he'd set. His line rang and rang, but he didn't pick up. I wiped the phone down and placed it back into my pocket. Then, I took my phone and slid it into the shirt pocket of the Polo that Percy was wearing. Before I'd bound and brought him to the Onyx, I'd dressed him in a pair of my clothes and underwear. Clothes that I'd sweated out.

I figured that not only would the Feds find my teeth in the aftermath of the fire, but they'd also find my DNA and my cell phone. Locust was stupid enough to put the word out to the Crips that if Percy didn't sign the papers and drop the $100,000 like he was supposed to, that his crew was going to burn the club to the ground. I was also sure that he'd let his crew know that I'd taken over the club and I swore that I was going to be there. I felt the smartest thing to do was to use his ignorance against him.

I heard a loud bang somewhere off in the club, and it was followed by a whoosh. The there was another bang, and it followed the same sound effects. I got up to go and look out of Percy's big managerial window, and saw that the downstairs to the club had been set ablaze. I smiled and nodded, walking over to Percy after taking out my lighter, leaning into his face.

"Well, I guess this is where you burn in hell, my nigga. I'll see you on the other side." I flicked the lighter and his face caught fire first, and then in less than a second his whole body was ablaze. I pushed the desk on top of him and ran out of the office, down the stairs, and ultimately out of the backdoor of the club. Before I was able to break free, I noted that there were big flames consuming the Onyx.

* * *

Myeesha was waiting for me in the truck when I made it into the alley. I jumped in and she pulled away in a haste. "You sure this is going to work, Jayden?" She looked over to me with a worried expression on her face.

I shrugged. "We ain't got not other choice now. Let's just get back, get this money, and keep it moving. You got all of his combinations?"

She nodded as she pulled onto the highway and stepped on the gas. "Yep, every single one of them. It ain't gon' be nothing to open those safes and get the cash out. What are we going to do after that though? What do I tell people when they ask where he is?" She looked over to me and then back to the road again. I could tell that she was very scared.

"You tell them that he'll be back. He never tells you where he goes or what he does, and they gon' have to respect that. Besides, how much longer are you planning on being in Atlanta?"

She shrugged. "I don't know, but now that his ass is out of the way, it opens up a list of opportunities, not only for myself, but for you and Miah as well. I can see that she has dreams and aspirations. I want to do the absolute best that I can to bring all of them to fruition. She deserves a good life, and for once I'll be able to focus in on her to the best of my ability. I owe her that." She sighed.

"Yo, it's been taking all the restraint that I got inside of me to not bust yo' ass for allowing that nigga to do nearly do anything that he wanted to my lil' cousin too. She told me how he forced her to go down on him a few times. She also said that the nigga tried to take the pussy right in front of you and you ain't even help to get him off of her. I couldn't believe my ears because I thought you were more of a protector than that."

She shook her head. "That's not entirely true, Jayden, and you should know that I would never allow for nobody to hurt my little sister. I've always stood up for her." She exhaled and switched lanes, speeding ahead of a green pickup truck that had a washing machine in the back of it. The driver beeped their horn.

Looking in the rear-view mirror, I could see him holding his fist in the air and shaking it in anger at us. "Yo, so why don't you tell me what's good then? Why would she say something like that?"

Myeesha shrugged. "I don't know, but we may have to sit down with her to find that out. Percy and Miah used to have a nice relationship before we moved into his mansion. He'd pick her up from school and take her shopping all the time, spending large sums of money on her. Long as he was doing that, everything was fine. They'd hug, there was even some harmless kissing every now and then, and I didn't think it was really a big deal. Then one day, after the SZA concert about four months back, we all came home, smoked a little of that Cuban reefer that Percy be having, drank a bottle of Seagram's Gin, getting a lil' tipsy, and Percy proposed that we have a threesome. Well, you already know how our DNA is set up. As long as Miah was down with it, then so was I. I asked her if she thought it was cool, and she nodded like it was no big deal, even walked over to him and kissed him right on the lips, jumped and wrapped her legs around him. Shit, he carried her upstairs to our master bedroom and left me downstairs feeling left out and stupid. I felt like they didn't even need me. That him proposing for us to have a threesome was all so he could get to fuck her lil' ass, and once again, I was cool with it."

I grunted and adjusted my shoulders uncomfortably. I was getting heated as I listened to her story. I didn't like imagining Percy's bitch ass touching Miah in no way. That punk disgusted me. "Yo, if you saying this shit happened like four months ago, that mean Miah was only seventeen. You let that fuck nigga put his nasty ass hands on her when she was still just a shorty." I said, still imagining Miah wrapping her legs around Percy's punk ass like she'd done me. I honestly felt kind of jealous more than anything.

Myeesha nodded, then shrugged. "I don't know what I was thinking that night. I see now that I was bogus and I should have broken it up. But that gin was getting the best of me, and I was horny, so I was down to go along with everything. I mean, I just gotta be honest." She turned on her blinker then swerved over two lanes, getting ready to get off on the next exit. I could see all of the color seem to leave her face as she replayed that night over in her mind's eye. "Damn, now you got me regretting that shit. I didn't even stop to think that she was only seventeen, Jayden. Fuck!"

"Yeah, well it's too late to dwell on that shit now. What happened that night? Don't lie to me either." I frowned and continued to watch her closely. I noticed that she couldn't stop fidgetting in her seat. She had this worried look on her face that I'd never seen before. "I'd never lie to you, and you know that." She mugged me and reduced her speeds as she entered on to the exit ramp. "Well, I didn't get up there until about ten minutes after they went ahead of me. When I got up there, Percy was on top of her, sucking her breasts. He was already naked, and Miah still had on her Fendi skirt and panties. When I stepped into the room, I was so drunk that I was staggering all over the place. Miah told me to come over and get him off of her, but I just figured that she wasn't serious. I don't know why I thought that, but like I said I was fucked up. So, I didn't help her. In fact, I slumped to the couch and sat my ass on it, trying my damnest to keep my eyes opened, and that was a task."

"So, then she was telling the truth. She asked you to help her and you didn't. That's bullshit." I snapped, ready to backhand her ass.

She shook her head, pulled up to the red light, and lowered it into her lap. "I blanked out, and when I woke up she was sucking his dick. Then, I passed back out. When I awoke the second time, he was there in the room sleep and she was gone over to her friends' Kenya and Kellis' house. We never spoke about that night and I never asked what happened after I passed out." The light flipped green, and the cars behind us tapped on their horn to let us know to drive off.

I blew air threw my teeth and shook my head in disgust. "Dude bitch ass got off on my lil' cousin, and you fell asleep. I oughta spank yo' lil' yellow ass. You know she told me that dude forced her to go down on him twice, so after that night, he must've went in on her again. I'm glad I fucked that nigga over. Miah might not ever be the same again. It's probably why she ain't fucked with nothing but females ever since then."

"You mean other than you right? Because I know you fucked her, didn't you?"

I nodded. "Yeah, we got it in a few times."

Myeesha flared her nostrils. "Yeah, I figured that. Well, hopefully he ain't screw her up too bad. I can't believe that I didn't even stop to think about that night, or what might have transpired between them after that. I done had my head so wrapped around hitting him for all of his money that I never stopped to think about that." She pulled up to the gate and Felix stepped out of the guard shack, and tilted his hat at her before opening the gate for us to enter.

"Tell Percy that he owes me for that Golden State series. I told him that New Orleans wouldn't get more than a game. Tell him I want my money, ASAP." He laughed, then walked back into his shack.

I mugged his bitch ass. I still remembered how he'd acted toward me on the first day that we'd met. We locked eyes, and I noted that his face went from that of cheer to a scowl. I wanted to jump out of the car and pistol-whip his wanna be tough ass.

Myeesha waved to him. "I'll make sure I tell him exactly that. He should be home in a few hour. Maybe you can tell him yourself, seeing as you'll see him down here before I see him back at the mansion." She slowly eased off of the brake, causing the car to move forward.

He never took his eyes away from me. His scowl became an intense mug. "Yeah, maybe I'll do just that. Have a good night. And you too, Jayden."

As soon as I heard my name leave his lips, a chill went down my spine, and the hairs on my arms stood on end. Myeesha pulled the whip down the winding road in silence. I didn't think she'd caught what had just taken place. "Yo, you told Felix that my name was Mark, right?" I looked into my rear-view mirror and saw him standing up at his guard shack, watching our whip.

"Yeah, but I only told him that because I didn't want him to know who you really were because of all that shit that took place back in Philly. People in Atlanta are nosey. All it takes is for the slightest bit of information to come out and they'll be able to tell you where you were born and what time your mother pushed you out. It's annoying. Why did you ask me that?"

I scrunched my face. "Because that punk just called me Jayden, then looked me in the eyes as if to say that he knew what was good with me. Should I be worried?"

Myeesha drove with both of her hands on the steering wheel, looking into her rear-view mirror with her eyesbrows raised. "I don't know, to be honest with you. I say we just get in here, pack up and get the fuck out of the A."

I lowered my head and exhaled. "Fuck. Yeah, let's just do that."

Myeesha pulled the whip into the driveway and we both seemed to jump out of it at the same time, jogging to the mansion's side entrance where she took out her key, and let us in. "Look, I'm going down to the basement, so I can empty out these safes. You go upstairs and get your things together, so we can be out of here first thing in the morning. I don't know where we're going to go as of yet, but you, me and Miah have to get the hell out of the A. Something ain't right. I can feel it in my bones."

I nodded. "Aiight, well, I'ma do just that. I'll be downstairs to help you in a minute." I jogged up the stairs, taking them two at a time until I got to the top and made my way down the hall. I kept on hearing Felix's bitch ass call me by my name. I saw his eyes as they peered into my own, Giving me a knowing look. I just wondered what it was that he really knew. Was it just my name?

Did he know about my past in Philly? Or was he conscious of the destruction that I'd caused ever since I'd touched down in Atlanta? Who had put him up on game? Even more than that, what was he going to do with the information that he'd discovered? My mind was racing a mile a second, and I felt sick to my stomach. I had to get the fuck out of Georgia and fast.

I jogged down the hallway, got to the guest bedroom door and pushed it open. The first thing I noticed was that the lights were out in the room. I found that odd off the back because before I'd left Percy's mansion I remembered that the lights had been on. I was in there counting my paper before I knocked Percy out and drug him down the stairs, unless Miah had gotten home, and thought to turn them off.

I took three steps to my right and flipped the switch. As soon as I did, I almost threw up all over the floor. There was a room full of masked men with all of their guns aimed at me, and sitting on the leather chair directly in front of them was Kilroy. He was the only one without a mask. Between his legs, and on her knees, was a duct taped Miah. She had tears flowing down her cheeks, and I could hear her whimpering through the tape.

I went to reach for the .45 at my waistband, and felt that it was not there. I'd left it in the car. I felt sick.

Kilroy grabbed Miah's hair roughly and yanked her head back. "All this time I thought you was a stomp down ass nigga but you wasn't nothing but a back-stabbing fuck nigga that gave my city of Philly a bad rep." He frowned and pulled a sharp knife out of the holster from inside of his fatigue jacket, placing the ridged blade to Miah neck, looking up at me with hatred.

I made a move to run over to him, and all at once I could hear the guns of his goons being cocked as they each took a step forward in protection of him.

"That ain't what you wanna do, kid. Word is bond, I'll have the Shooters light yo' ass up like the fourth of July." Kilroy said, sliding the blade slightly across Miah's neck, just enough to make her draw a thick line of blood.

She screamed into the tape as tears dripped off of her chin.

I felt my heart sink. I held my hands in the air. "Yo, nigga, I'm right here. Whatever you wanna do to me, you can do it. Just let her go. She ain't got shit to do with this. This Philly business." I looked into his eyes and clenched my jaw. I hated that I'd left my pistol in the car, because had I not I would've made them gun me down. The fact that Kilroy had already caused my lil' cousin to bleed meant that he was going to kill her. I knew how he got down; she didn't have a chance. He was bred by the slums of Philly, which meant the nigga was heartless.

He mugged me. "Bitch nigga, ain't you the same muthafucka that killed my right hand man because he found out about you and Shawn fucking around behind Naz's back?" He lowered his eyes into slits and pursed his lips.

I exhaled and knew it was over. "Man, who the fuck told you some bullshit like that? That was my lil' nigga, and you know it." I said, trying to think of a plan in my head, but nothing was coming to the forefront.

"Bitch nigga, as soon as it happened he texted me about it. Then on top of that, that bitch told me. So as far as I'm concerned, it's an eye for an eye." He yanked Miah's hair back, stabbed the knife into the side of her neck, and drug it across once, and then all the way back again.

Her blood spat into the air before her eyes crossed, and he threw her to the floor aggressively. I watched the carpet fill up with her blood while she jerked and shook.

Kilroy nodded. "Yeah, fuck nigga, it's your turn now. Get his ass."

Before I could even think about it, I spun on the balls of my feet, ducked and made my way toward the open door as the shots rang out in my direction.

Boom. Boom. Boom. Boom. Big chunks of the drywall exploded by my head. A bullet slammed into my back, and another one into the right side of my shoulder, knocking me forward. It felt like acid was being poured into me. My vision got blurry immediately, but it didn't stop me from running as fast as I could as more bullet struck my flesh, one after the other.

Now I could barely breathe. I felt my blood pouring out of me. I could feel air going into the holes in my back, and the bullets swimming around inside of me. I made it to the top of the stairs and fell down them. The room blinked in and out. My vision had lost every color of its detail, except that of the color red. I struggled to get to my feet as more and more shots rang out. I needed to get downstairs so I could save Myeesha. I couldn't allow for her to meet the same fate that Miah had. I was wishing that I'd never come to Atlanta. That I'd never brought this drama their way. They would have been better off without ever knowing me.

Boo-wa! I felt the shotgun blast punch a hole through my left thigh, buckling me. I fell onto my stomach and crawled to the top of the basement steps, and forced myself to fall down them as I had the other flight. *Duh-duh-duh-duh!* I rolled down them, landing on my bloodied back, coughing up my own blood.

Kilroy stopped at the top of them with a shotgun in his hand. He looked down on me and made his way into the basement with a smile on his face. "Yo, niggas, chill. I'm gon' be the one to finish his ass off. Karma is a muthafucka." He said, coming down the stairs slowly.

I was struggling to breathe. Blood poured out of my mouth and blocked my airways. I turned onto my side and cough, spitting a bunch of it onto the concrete. I looked up and saw Felix with his hand around Myeesha's throat, and a .9-millimeter pressed against her forehead. Behind him, all three safes were opened, along with a Louis Vuitton suitcase full of what I imagined to be my money.

"What's good, Jayden? I bet you ain't expect shit to end like this, huh?" He laughed, turned to Myeesha and curled his lip. "It's been fun, but money rules everything around me." *Boom.*

Her head jerked on her neck before he let her go, and she sank to the ground with half of her head blown off.

All of the fight slowly left my body. Kilroy came over and flipped me over, putting the shotgun into my eye socket like I'd done so many niggas in the past. It felt ironic that I found myself on the receiving end. I didn't understand how everything crumbled around me so fast. I struggled to get air into my lungs. I was ready to die and go out like I deserved, but I just had to know how my demise came to be.

So, with the bit of breath that I had left, I found the strength to ask my last question. "How did you find me?" The beats in my heart got weaker and weaker. The room began to spin. I could see the angel of death standing in the corner of the basement, right behind the open safes. I felt my blood oozing down my neck, and the bullets in my back felt as if they were still spinning and spewing acid deep within me. I was in so much pain that I welcomed death.

Felix laughed and aimed his gun down at me. "Percy was a coward. He knew that he'd have to get rid of you eventually, so he kept his ear to the streets of Philly."

"Yeah, and that nigga found out that I put two hunnit bands on yo' head. Instead of him killing you and taking the money, he offered the contract to Felix over here." Kilroy said.

"Yeah, and before I handled that business, I figured it'd be in my best interest to touch bases with him to make sure that everything was everything. Once he found out that I knew where you were, he offered to hit me with two hunnit bands just for your location, had one fifty dropped off to me up front, and told me to not touch a hair on your head, so I didn't. By that time, me and Myeesha were already plotting on how to knock off Percy anyway. She knew Kilroy and his crew were coming to kill you, and she didn't even—"

Boo-wa! Kilroy had raised his shotgun and blew Felix's head clean off his neck. I watched him fall to his knees, and then fall onto his chest, with blood spurting out of him.

"That nigga talk too much. It's Philly or nothing anyway." He laughed and pressed the hot barrel of the shotgun into my right eye. "Any last words, my nigga?"

I kicked my legs and struggled to breathe, swallowing more and more of my own blood, wheezing loudly. "Fuck you!"

Kilroy laughed and lowered his eyes. "Rest in peace, you rotten ass nigga."

Boo-wa!

The End!

Submission Guideline

Submit the first three chapters of your completed manuscript to ldpsubmissions@gmail.com, subject line: Your book's title. The manuscript must be in a .doc file and sent as an attachment. Document should be in Times New Roman, double spaced and in size 12 font. Also, provide your synopsis and full contact information. If sending multiple submissions, they must each be in a separate email.

Have a story but no way to send it electronically? You can still submit to LDP/Ca$h Presents. Send in the first three chapters, written or typed, of your completed manuscript to:

LDP: Submissions Dept
Po Box 870494
Mesquite, Tx 75187

DO NOT send original manuscript. Must be a duplicate.

Provide your synopsis and a cover letter containing your full contact information.

Thanks for considering LDP and Ca$h Presents.

Coming Soon from Lock Down Publications/Ca$h Presents

BOW DOWN TO MY GANGSTA
By **Ca$h**
TORN BETWEEN TWO
By **Coffee**
BLOOD STAINS OF A SHOTTA **III**
By **Jamaica**
STEADY MOBBIN II
By **Marcellus Allen**
BLOOD OF A BOSS **V**
By **Askari**
LOYAL TO THE GAME **IV**
By **T.J. & Jelissa**
A DOPEBOY'S PRAYER **II**
By **Eddie "Wolf" Lee**
IF LOVING YOU IS WRONG… **III**
LOVE ME EVEN WHEN IT HURTS
By **Jelissa**
TRUE SAVAGE **V**
By **Chris Green**
BLAST FOR ME **III**
By **Ghost**
ADDICTIED TO THE DRAMA **III**
By **Jamila Mathis**
LIPSTICK KILLAH **III**
CRIME OF PASSION **II**

By **Mimi**

WHAT BAD BITCHES DO **III**

KILL ZONE

By **Aryanna**

THE COST OF LOYALTY **II**

By **Kweli**

SHE FELL IN LOVE WITH A REAL ONE **II**

By **Tamara Butler**

LOVE SHOULDN'T HURT **III**

RENEGADE BOYS **II**

By **Meesha**

CORRUPTED BY A GANGSTA **III**

By **Destiny Skai**

A GANGSTER'S CODE III

By **J-Blunt**

KING OF NEW YORK III

By **T.J. Edwards**

CUM FOR ME **IV**

By **Ca$h & Company**

GORILLAS IN THE BAY

De'Kari

THE STREETS ARE CALLING

Duquie Wilson

Available Now

RESTRAINING ORDER **I & II**

Ghost

By **Meesha**

A GANGSTER'S CODE I & II

By J-Blunt

PUSH IT TO THE LIMIT

By **Bre' Hayes**

BLOOD OF A BOSS **I, II, III & IV**

By **Askari**

THE STREETS BLEED MURDER **I, II & III**

THE HEART OF A GANGSTA I II& III

By **Jerry Jackson**

CUM FOR ME

CUM FOR ME 2

CUM FOR ME 3

An **LDP Erotica Collaboration**

BRIDE OF A HUSTLA **I II & II**

THE FETTI GIRLS **I, II& III**

CORRUPTED BY A GANGSTA I & II

By **Destiny Skai**

WHEN A GOOD GIRL GOES BAD

By **Adrienne**

A GANGSTER'S REVENGE **I II III & IV**

THE BOSS MAN'S DAUGHTERS

THE BOSS MAN'S DAUGHTERS II

THE BOSSMAN'S DAUGHTERS III

THE BOSSMAN'S DAUGHTERS IV

THE BOSS MAN'S DAUGHTERS **V**

A SAVAGE LOVE **I & II**

BAE BELONGS TO ME

A HUSTLER'S DECEIT I, II

WHAT BAD BITCHES DO I, II

By **Aryanna**

A KINGPIN'S AMBITON

A KINGPIN'S AMBITION **II**

I MURDER FOR THE DOUGH

By **Ambitious**

TRUE SAVAGE

TRUE SAVAGE II

TRUE SAVAGE **III**

TRUE SAVAGE **IV**

By **Chris Green**

A DOPEBOY'S PRAYER

By **Eddie "Wolf" Lee**

THE KING CARTEL **I, II & III**

By **Frank Gresham**

THESE NIGGAS AIN'T LOYAL **I, II & III**

By **Nikki Tee**

GANGSTA SHYT **I II &III**

By **CATO**

THE ULTIMATE BETRAYAL

By **Phoenix**

BOSS'N UP **I , II & III**

By **Royal Nicole**

I LOVE YOU TO DEATH

By Destiny J

I RIDE FOR MY HITTA

I STILL RIDE FOR MY HITTA

By **Misty Holt**

LOVE & CHASIN' PAPER

By **Qay Crockett**

TO DIE IN VAIN

By **ASAD**

BROOKLYN HUSTLAZ

By **Boogsy Morina**

BROOKLYN ON LOCK I & II

By **Sonovia**

GANGSTA CITY

By **Teddy Duke**

A DRUG KING AND HIS DIAMOND I & II III

A DOPEMAN'S RICHES

By Nicole Goosby

TRAPHOUSE KING **I II & III**

By **Hood Rich**

LIPSTICK KILLAH **I, II**

CRIME OF PASSION

By **Mimi**

STEADY MOBBN'

By **Marcellus Allen**

WHO SHOT YA **I, II**

Renta

BOOKS BY LDP'S CEO, CA$H

TRUST IN NO MAN

TRUST IN NO MAN 2

TRUST IN NO MAN 3

BONDED BY BLOOD

SHORTY GOT A THUG

THUGS CRY

THUGS CRY 2

THUGS CRY 3

TRUST NO BITCH

TRUST NO BITCH 2

TRUST NO BITCH 3

TIL MY CASKET DROPS

RESTRAINING ORDER

RESTRAINING ORDER 2

IN LOVE WITH A CONVICT

Coming Soon

BONDED BY BLOOD 2

BOW DOWN TO MY GANGSTA

www.ingramcontent.com/pod-product-compliance
Lightning Source LLC
Chambersburg PA
CBHW070025260626

47159CB00005B/1952